### Praise for *Working Class Boy*

'When *Working Class Boy* came out, I hailed it as a classic of Australian biography. Nearly a decade later, I haven't changed my mind. By every measure I care about, Barnes's book was a piece of literature. The purpose of literature, said Joseph Conrad, is "by the power of the written word, to make you hear, to make you feel – it is, above all, to make you see". Barnes's memoir did all those things' – David Free, *Sydney Morning Herald*

'*Working Class Boy* is a stunning piece of work – relentless, earnest, shockingly vivid. Barnes … doesn't just have a scarifying story to tell. He has a grippingly effective way of telling it: one that does full justice to the grim facts without overcooking them … You can't fake such a tone. You have to earn it' – *The Australian*

'Nothing will prepare you for the power of Jimmy's memoir. A fierce, graphic, bawdy account of his working-class childhood – truly harrowing, and yet often tender and funny. I couldn't put it down because, above all, it is also a story of resilience and bravery' – Sam Neill

'Visceral, brave, honest. A deep, guttural howl of a book, it speaks of the pain and hurt that haunt so many men. And it may just save lives' – Magda Szubanski

'Barnes writes with verve and style to present a fascinating story of flawed and compelling personalities, not least his own. The result is unexpectedly compelling' – *Rolling Stone*

'Barnes's way of addressing the reader directly, while largely ignoring his rock-star status, edges towards a unique voice' – *The Listener*

## Praise for *Working Class Man*

'All the mind-boggling excesses and the emotional extremes are revealed here, with brutal honesty and sparkling wit. Jimmy has found his real voice, and it's imbued with a spirit of generosity that knows no bounds – just like the man himself' – Neil Finn

'What a brave writer ... The legend who strides the stage with so much power and charisma reveals the boy who hid in a cupboard then found salvation in song, the rock star who had it all and spent it all, and the man who loves his family and his music' – Lindy Morrison

'Jimmy has always been a force of nature, living on the edge, giving high-octane performances ... Yet, as this book shows, his wrestle with his hidden demons was taking a huge toll. Something had to give, and this searingly honest account lays it out in spades' – Peter Garrett

'A story as dark as pitch but so compelling, so powerful and at times so close to unbelievable – how can this man still be alive? – it sets a new bar for rock 'n' roll survival stories ... What lifts this memoir is its searing honesty, and Jimmy's tender, sincere regret for what the circus he ringmastered did to his own wife and family. Also to himself' – Jennifer Byrne, *Australian Women's Weekly*

'Only a fool would declare the circus animal's rage spent. But in these two books, he's broken it down and owned every part of it with the kind of honesty, clear-eyed insight and riveting storytelling that miraculously defies the damage done' – Michael Dwyer, *Sydney Morning Herald*

**Praise for *Killing Time***

'Features the same immersive storytelling that readers and music fans have come to know him for. Ranging from charming, to witty, to entirely heartbreaking, the tales are brief snapshots into one of the most storied and accomplished lives in Australian music' – *Rolling Stone*

'A moving and deeply felt kaleidoscope of life, love, family, music, friendship and the fragility of time. Barnes proved his storytelling mettle with his memoirs. But in *Killing Time* he has refined his unique voice with this wildly entertaining suite of tales, anecdotes, observations and reflections that can have you laughing out loud on one page and moved to tears on the next. It is all here, the joys and fears of parenthood, the search for your sense of place, fortune-tellers, the loss of beloved pets, bad golf, ghosts, backstage stories, celebrities, the homeless, and the wonder of being alive, all told with searing honesty. What sets Barnes's writing above the rest is that it comes from an authentic and soulful place. His work cannot help but ring true, like the strike of a tuning fork' – Matt Condon

'Jimmy Barnes is never a bystander. Stories happen to him. He not only remembers every circumstance, he has the ability to distil the moment in a way that's both poetic and uncontrived. He's funny, chaotic, insightful and heartbreaking. Jimmy is truly a natural-born storyteller. It's like writing has just been waiting for him to arrive. And now, he's here' – Mandy Nolan

# Jimmy Barnes

## Highways AND Byways

HarperCollins*Publishers*

www.jimmybarnes.com

🅕 🅞 : @jimmybarnesofficial

🅧 : @jimmybarnes

Management: Mahalia Barnes for Working Class Management
Mahalia@applestreetmusic.com

**HarperCollins**_Publishers_
Australia • Brazil • Canada • France • Germany • Holland • India
Italy • Japan • Mexico • New Zealand • Poland • Spain • Sweden
Switzerland • United Kingdom • United States of America

HarperCollins acknowledges the Traditional Custodians
of the lands upon which we live and work, and pays respect
to Elders past and present.

First published on Gadigal Country in Australia in 2024
by HarperCollins_Publishers_ Australia Pty Limited
ABN 36 009 913 517
harpercollins.com.au

A catalogue record for this book is available from the National Library of Australia

ISBN 978 1 4607 6672 9 (hardback)
ISBN 978 1 4607 1800 1 (ebook)
ISBN 978 1 4607 3048 5 (audiobook)

Cover design by HarperCollins Design Studio
Cover images and the photographs on pages viii, xvii, xviii, xix and 294–295 © Jesse Lizotte
Endpaper images by istockphoto.com
All images from the Barnes family archive unless otherwise noted
Typeset in Bembo Std by Kirby Jones
Printed and bound in Australia by McPherson's Printing Group

MIX
Paper | Supporting
responsible forestry
FSC
www.fsc.org    FSC® C001695

*To the love of my life, my Jane,*
*and to my beautiful children,*
*grandchildren and great-grandchildren*

# Contents

# Introduction

It seems that I always start writing after some sort of health scare raises its ugly head. I struggle with ADHD, and it has become obvious to me that unless I am bedridden and can't move, I have way too much on my plate to sit still long enough to write anything more than a thank-you note. This time round, my calendar was suddenly cleared for months on end from late 2023, thanks to a friendly little staph infection that wanted to kill me, which led to two rounds of surgery, including open-heart surgery. Once again, I was stuck flat on my back, with a lot of time for reading, which, as it usually does, encouraged me to start writing again. There's an old Scottish phrase, 'What's fur ye will no go by ye', which basically means if something's meant to be, then it will be. So I accepted the situation, told myself I was meant to be writing, and started a new book. The title is somewhat ironic, as the only highways and byways I could visit were in my head.

Ever since my first memoir, *Working Class Boy,* reading and writing have helped me get back on my feet metaphorically, but this time it was true, literally. Telling these stories provided a much-needed focus as I rebuilt my concentration and strength. Reading both inspired and consoled me, especially reading the many letters of sympathy and support I received. I'm truly grateful for all of them, and they were a timely reminder of how words can help us all heal.

I soon slipped into a daily routine – not the familiar loud rhythms of travel–soundcheck–gig–travel that I've known since I was in my teens, but a new regime of early morning physio and exercise near our home, followed by a few hours of sitting in silence, sipping coffee and writing at my desk. I was itching to return to the rock 'n' roll life I know best, of course, but it still felt good to get back into some kind of groove. Not surprisingly, most of the first stories I wrote involved travelling. It would be months before I could hit the road again and reconnect face to face with friends, family and fans around Australia and overseas, but in the meantime I could at least scratch my itchy feet by reliving some memorable and amusing trips from earlier years.

As my near-death experience gradually receded in the rearview mirror, I started to put it into perspective and found myself driven to share more obscure stories from a past I had nearly lost. Revisiting some key episodes in my life, in writing, was my way of getting my bearings as my family and I navigated our way out of a very upsetting period. I would turn the pages in my memory to see what could be mined from them and be surprised to discover some gems I wanted to share. So many lost things were now easy to find, as if my health scare had somehow drawn those memories closer to the surface. Stories I had touched on in previous books came through to me in more detail. Memories that the first time round had left me white knuckled, squeezing the arms of my chair and sitting staring at the pages in front of me with knots in my stomach, now opened up to me in new ways. I could see why certain moments constantly resurfaced. There was more to learn.

Retracing your life in this way helps you track all the twists and turns you took to get to where you are today, revealing how they have all contributed to *who* you are. These routes are the highways and byways of life, the main roads and the detours – the times you knew exactly where you were going, and the moments when you felt completely lost, as well as the paths you didn't even realise you'd followed.

Generally speaking, the highways in these stories are the parts of my life that played out in public, the moments where things went right or wrong in ways that taught me something or made me laugh. Many of the more interesting experiences have occurred on the byways, though – in small, unseen places out of the spotlight, where I discovered things I didn't expect, and things I'll never forget.

This time around, I also wanted to experiment with different ways of recording and reflecting on my experiences. Having the rug pulled from under my feet always seems to trigger some of the most epic journeys anyone can take – the ones that happen between the ears. Whenever the harsh realities of life have entrapped me, my mind has run away to places I'm unlikely to ever visit. As a child, if I was sick in bed, I would rocket through space to distant galaxies and sail across stormy oceans to do battle with fearful monsters. Whenever I felt unsafe at home and the fighting of my mum and dad got too much to handle, I could just close my eyes and let my mind take me to, say, the mountains of Japan, where, dressed in samurai clothes, I would jump from roofs, wield razor-sharp swords and defend castles from evil ninjas.

As I grew a bit older, I escaped into books and films instead; then came music, plus some other strategies that weren't as healthy. It wasn't until the last decade or so that I again started retreating to the safety and wonder of my imagination. As I began to sort through childhood traumas, the ability to see past events through the eyes of an outside observer served me well. I could relive the pain and hurt without it taking such a toll. In fact, using my imagination to make myself hover above situations allowed me to examine them and then let them go.

So, in these new stories I wanted to explore that freedom I'd rediscovered, let my writing roam further afield. I found I could invoke memories, then let my imagination take over. As a result, *Highways and Byways* is a collection of stories from my travels with my family and my band, mixed up with some more fanciful tales that the child in me can still conjure up. The lines between fact and fiction are sometimes sharp, but at other times they're well and truly blurred, by design. I will leave you to try to figure out which ones are which.

Music has, of course, been an inspiration and a guide throughout every single one of these journeys. I'm constantly compiling lists of favourite songs and, as recounted in these pages, I have always enjoyed a good mix tape, or playlist as they're known these days. So, alongside some of these stories, I've shared lists of songs and other musical compositions that I've long loved and sometimes performed, music that often transports me back to the particular time or place featured in that chapter. I hope the playlists will inspire you to investigate and enjoy some of these tracks, and maybe even compile lists of your own. We all know that nothing unlocks memories like music and that every story is improved by the right soundtrack, and I hope that's the case here too.

As the beautiful photos taken by my dear nephew Jesse Lizotte for the cover of this book show, I'm still a proud Scot, even though I left there when I was a little boy. The sound of bagpipes and the taste of 'tatties' have often provided solace over the years, as if they are somehow hardwired into my DNA. I don't think it's a coincidence that our much-loved home outside Sydney is in an area known as 'The Highlands'. Of course, the Scots have proud literary and musical traditions – our folk songs bind us. Like I said in my first book, they allow us to emigrate to far-flung places and then spend the rest of our lives drinking whisky and singing about how much we miss Scotland!

Arguably one of Scotland's signature folk songs is 'The Bonnie Banks o' Loch Lomond'. It features a famous chorus that I have sung many times at drunken parties and family gatherings, and even after the passing of my dear friend Jock Zonfrillo:

> O ye'll tak' the high road and I'll tak' the low road,
> and I'll be in Scotland afore ye …

Whichever road we choose to take, I've learned that the way to escape tough times is to travel back to our special places – wherever and whenever they might have been – and reconsider how we got from there to where we are now. In doing so, we can find gratitude for every extra day we get to share, exploring more highways and byways together.

Jimmy

# Highways
## AND Byways

# A Visit from Steve

I am driving a van that is cruising down the highway en route to one of the first of the Cold Chisel fiftieth-anniversary shows.

The band are all with me, sitting in the back – Don, Ian, Phil and Charley – and the level of excitement is high. This is the first show of the latest tour, a tour that sold out in minutes, and we can't wait to get on stage and tear into some rock 'n' roll. After all, that's what we do best, make music, and playing live shows is what we live for.

It seems like only yesterday that the seat now occupied by Charley Drayton, one of the best groove drummers in the world, was filled by our dear friend Steve Prestwich. Steve was a tall, gentle Liverpudlian who could drive a band better than anyone I knew. I grew up close to Steve. We came from similar backgrounds, declining British industrial cities, and our families came to Australia for similar reasons – in search of a better life, in search of a future.

When Steve joined Cold Chisel, on a fateful day in 1973, we became friends forever. And even as the friendship grew, he and I managed to push all the right buttons in each other – and in others – to give us the edge we needed to propel the band into the stratosphere.

Aside from Steve and me, all the band members came from different walks of life, so the influences that drove our group were as diverse and different as our upbringings. Ian, a country boy from Alice Springs, brought blistering hot guitars with a wide open sound, reminiscent of the big country he came from. Don Walker, a complex man, who thought long and hard before making decisions, brought strength and melody, and shared a deep knowledge of music that profoundly influenced the rest of us. Phil was a quiet achiever, who, despite his gentle demeanour, played driving basslines that were both melodic and powerful. Steve's innate sense of rhythm and melody became a huge asset as the band developed and his songwriting came to the forefront. As for me, I always felt my job was to be the conduit, the person who reached out to the audience and offered them a way to connect with us and come along for the ride.

Ten years of touring and laughing flew by, and it came time for Cold Chisel to take a rest. But it wouldn't be for long. We just couldn't stay apart. It wasn't just about friendship or the shared struggles we'd gone through as young men, it was also about the music we were all devoted to. We knew we still had many songs to write, many shows to play.

But then, in 2011, in a blow so painful we thought it would bring down everything we had built up, we lost Steve to a brain tumour. It was shattering to lose our bandmate, our friend, and it took us several years to come to terms with the loss. We had no idea how to move on, yet every time we got together, we realised we still had unfinished business. Eventually, we were lucky enough to find Charley Drayton, who graciously agreed to sit in the drummer's seat. Not only has he filled the hole that was left after Steve's passing, but in his own way he has also powered us to bigger and better things. Yet Steve is always right there in our hearts every time we go on stage.

On the drive today, the radio constantly plays and music from our past drifts through the van, heightening our sense of anticipation. The feeling between the members of the band is good – it's been too long since we last played together. Suddenly, a song comes on the radio that we all know well. It's 'Flame Trees', written by Steve and Don. It's one of the best we ever recorded, a crowd favourite, and it always takes me back to those days when we were young and the whole world lay before us, waiting to be experienced. Every time I sing it, I think of Steve, and tears fill my eyes.

The song on the radio is not the band's version, however; it's my slower, more melodramatic rendition, which I've been performing with my own band for the last few years. The van has gone quiet and I feel a bit embarrassed. I reach for the radio to turn it down, and blurt out, 'Sorry, guys. Why are they playing this version? It should be ours.'

But as my hand touches the dial, another hand gently reaches over and pulls it back. It's Steve. He's right there in the front passenger seat, next to me. I see him as clear as day, and his touch is warm and comforting.

'Leave it, Jim,' he says gently. 'It sounds great. You're singing it beautifully.'

Waiting for Steve to approve the groove, 1997. Left to right: Phil Small, Steve, Don Walker and me.

Then, all at once, it goes dark. I open my eyes and realise I'm in my bed. I turn to the clock. It's five in the morning.

I get up and go quietly to the kitchen to make coffee, trying not to wake anyone. I don't want to go back to sleep. I want to dwell on this moment alone, make it last. I want the feeling of my dear friend's hand on mine to stay. I want to keep Steve with me for as long as I can.

And I know then, as I stand alone in my kitchen, that the upcoming tour will be beautiful and that Steve will be with us, just as he always was.

# Trouble in the Rearview Mirror

Many years ago I wanted to buy a large, comfortable car. A few friends of mine said, 'What you need is the Mercedes 450 6.9 litre. It's big and it drives like a limo.'

I looked around and, as luck would have it, I found one for sale. That model hadn't been made for a couple of years, but the one I found was not very old and in great condition, so I snapped it up. Silver in colour, with really stylish lines, it looked good on me. It was called a Mercedes Pullman and was about twelve inches longer than a standard Mercedes 450, so it had plenty of room inside. Jane and I, the kids and the luggage all fitted quite comfortably, and we still had room for our dog, Theo, whenever we had to squeeze him in. Theo was a Labrador cross who, as he got older, looked like he had been crossed with a coffee table – he was huge and liked to stretch out across the kids.

I fitted the car with a state-of-the-art stereo. You know, the kind with lots of speakers and a subwoofer so powerful that it frightens pedestrians whenever you drive by. I also added some big wheels and tyres, comfortable and luxurious sheepskin covers on the seats for those long drives, and tinted the windows so that no one could see in – in fact it was hard to see out of it. Then I was ready to rock.

At the time we were living in the Southern Highlands of New South Wales, between the towns of Bowral and Mittagong. From there I had easy access to the freeway and could get to Sydney in an hour and a half or so, which was handy as I spent a lot of time working there. I loved driving while listening to music – it was one of my favourite things to do. In fact, I had already spent about thirty or so years doing just that. Well, not just that: we broke up our drives by doing blistering rock 'n' roll shows all across the country.

My stereo not only kicked arse but kicked everything else that came within thirty yards of it. It was so loud I thought I might have to drive with the windows wound down to avoid blowing them out. Luckily for me, the windows were armour-plate glass. Anyway, the biggest problem I had driving the car related to this very stereo. The louder I turned it up, the faster I seemed to drive. It was as if the volume had a direct connection to my right foot. And if AC/DC were playing, which was often the case, I couldn't seem to drive under 200 kilometres an hour. I realised that might be a problem if I encountered any police, but hoped that if I drove through a speed trap the car would be a blur and they wouldn't know what the hell had just passed them. In the meantime, I was in seventh heaven.

Everything went great until Cold Chisel decided that we would do a week's rehearsals in Sydney. Cold Chisel didn't rehearse a lot. We found it worked better if we snuck up on ourselves. The audience used to think that at times we were so out of control that we might not know what was going to happen next. But they misjudged us. We were so out of control we *never* knew what was happening next. In fact, quite often, even after the show had finished, I still didn't know what had happened just before.

But this week we were rehearsing. I think we must have been making a record, or something serious like that. Rather than stay in Sydney for the week, I decided to drive up there in the morning and back to the country every night. What could go wrong? I made up a bunch of mix tapes for the car. Remember cassettes? I used to stop and buy cassettes by obscure, sometimes dodgy-looking country artists at truck stops and play them in the car when I was sick of my own cassettes. If they passed the first-listen test, I'd often find them under the back seat months later when cleaning the car, sometimes with mysterious, Labrador-like bite marks on them. If they didn't pass the test, they were either gently placed in a bin on arrival at my destination or unceremoniously thrown from the car at high speed. So it was better if I made my own mix tapes. It was a hobby of mine.

I didn't have a lot of hobbies back then, partly because I had the attention span of a small soap dish and found it hard to concentrate on anything much at all. I collected butterflies – well, moths really – but they were stuck to the front grille of my car, so that didn't count as a hobby. I played golf, but giving a frustrated Scotsman a stick to swing at things is not really a good idea, so that was put on hold. I also tried to read as much as I could. Jane had introduced me to Shakespeare, astonished that I had never read any before. I gave it a go, but it always looked like it was written in another language. So Jane bought me *Tales from Shakespeare* by Charles and Mary Lamb. It was essentially Shakespeare for kids, but at least I could work out what he was saying. I didn't think he was any good – all much ado about nothing, you might say. (See what I did there? Because of jokes like that, Jane nearly gave up recommending books to me.)

Karate was another pastime I tried. It at least got me fit, which made our shows better, but it also turned me into the kind of guy you didn't want to meet in a dark alley. Or even a light alley, come to think of it. No, music has been my only hobby, I guess. It's been my love, my passion and pretty well everything to me since the moment I first heard Little Richard scream 'Tutti Frutti' through the distorting speaker of my transistor radio. And mix tapes had been something I liked to make for years.

I became restless as the rehearsals crept up on me. I was never any good at them because I was so impatient. The best thing about them for me was that most of the time we were in rooms with padded walls, so I could bang my head against them whenever I liked.

On the morning of the first rehearsal I was up early, ready to face the day. Jane fed me a big breakfast, probably because she knew it would be the last good thing I'd eat all day, kissed me on the cheek and waved goodbye from the front step. I couldn't work out why she looked so happy to see me leaving. As soon as the car started, she went inside and I hit the road. In fact that was name of the first song on my latest mix tape: 'Hit the Road Jack' by Ray Charles.

The sun was shining, the music was blaring, the highway lay in front of me and I had two hours or so until we started work. I had designed the tape so that when I pulled up outside the rehearsal studio it would be reaching a crescendo. 'Hit the Road Jack' led into 'Whole Lotta Shakin' Going On' by Jerry Lee Lewis, and by the time 'The Girl Can't Help It' by Little Richard reached its chorus I was flying down the freeway.

Soon after, though, I said to myself, 'I don't remember that sound in this song.'

I turned the music up and kept driving. Then I noticed that somebody was trying to pass me. That was unusual, as no one ever passed *me* on the freeway.

'That's a fast car,' I thought. 'Nice flashing light too … *Shit*, it's a cop.'

As he overtook me, he pointed to the side of the road.

'I think he wants me to stop,' I told myself. I looked over at him again. 'Yep, he definitely wants me to stop.'

I hit the brakes as the police car crossed in front of me and guided me to the side of the freeway.

'Should I stay in the car or jump out and meet him halfway?' I wondered.

I opted for the latter, but got out of the car so fast I was waiting at his door when he opened it. I think it gave him a bit of a start.

'Licence, please,' he said politely but firmly as he opened his notebook.

As he looked up, a slight smile appeared on his face, but he quickly wiped it and regained his composure before saying, 'Excuse me, sir, is your name Jimmy Barnes?'

'Yes, officer.'

He couldn't keep it together. 'You're that bloke from Cold Chisel,' he blurted excitedly.

'Yes, sir, that's me.'

'I'll let you in on a little secret, Jimmy. My wife and I danced to one of your songs at our wedding.'

'Oh yeah. Which one?'

'"Shipping Steel". Love that one.'

This was not the answer I'd expected. But I now thought there might be a chance I'd get away without a ticket.

'Do you know what speed you were doing, Jimmy?'

'No, to tell you the truth I didn't look. I was listening to truck-driving songs on the cassette player.' I thought this might appeal to his sense of humour.

It didn't. His face went sour. 'Yeah, that's funny, Jimmy. You were doing 210 kilometres an hour.'

'Really?'

'Yep, really. Can I have your licence, please.'

He opened his notebook and seemed to write for about ten minutes before he handed me a ticket.

'You'd better slow down a bit, mate, or you won't make it to your next show. You just lost six points from your licence. You've only got twelve. So take it easy.'

I sheepishly took the ticket, got back in the car, turned down the music, hit the indicator and pulled back out onto the freeway.

For the next few painful kilometres, I watched him in the rearview mirror as he followed behind me. I hadn't even realised that my super car could go this slow. It was a struggle to keep my speed below 110 kilometres an hour and avoid getting arrested. I really needed to play something that would help me drive slowly, but unfortunately my *Best of Leonard Cohen* tape seemed to be missing.

After about ten miserable minutes of watching the white line, I looked up again at the rearview mirror to find he was gone. Not a sign of him. He must have turned around and headed in the other direction in search of a new victim. Heaving a sigh of relief, I quickly pushed the cassette back into the player and turned the volume knob to warp speed. The unmistakable sound of The Sensational Alex Harvey Band filled the car and I immediately felt happier. My foot once again began trying to visit the floor. And who was I to argue with my own foot? My mood had taken a huge swing from 'Woe is me' to 'Let's make up some time, fast.'

But that was when I looked in the mirror again and saw, to my amazement, my friendly dancing policeman right there on my tail.

'Where did he come from?' I exclaimed.

I glanced down at the speedometer. Was it my imagination, or was I now pushing 240 Ks? 'Man, this car just gets real fast, real easy.'

By now the lights were flashing again and I knew I was in trouble. I pulled over to the side of the road, but this time I stayed in the car. He walked slowly up to my door and signalled to me to wind down the window. I pressed the button.

'Hi, officer.'

'You want to get out of the car, Jimmy? We need to talk.'

I stepped out of the car and stood with my head bowed, clearly a man full of remorse who had learned a lesson in life. A man who would probably never speed again.

'Was I speeding again?' I asked.

'Not only speeding again, but you were going faster than last time I pulled you over. Which, by the way, was less than ten kilometres back down the road.'

He pulled out his trusty notebook. I guessed he didn't want my autograph.

'This ticket brings your total loss of points for the day up to twelve, Jimmy. That means, technically, you can't drive again for a while. But since it's you, and since you have brought me so much joy over the years – I even learned to dance because of you – I will let you turn around and drive yourself home.'

This was disastrous. I needed to be at rehearsals and I needed to be there soon. I did everything but drop to my knees and plead the fifth. I promised him I would only drive to rehearsals, then straight home. I promised him that from now on my wife would be doing the driving, and I swore on my mother's grave that I would never speed again. I think that's what clinched it for me. (My mother was alive and well, by the way, and living next door to me, but I wasn't going to tell him that.)

He scratched his head. I could see the wheels turning and I knew he was considering letting me drive on. I gave him my most innocent-looking smile, the one I pull out only on special occasions.

He passed me the ticket and looked me in the eye. 'Go on, Jimmy. But when you get home tonight, that is it. You're finished, okay?'

'Yes, sir.'

I thanked him and jumped back into the Mercedes

before he could change his mind. As I drove off, I could see him standing beside his car wondering why he'd just agreed to that proposition.

I drove like a pensioner on quaaludes all the way to rehearsals. I was lucky to get there. We worked until about seven o'clock that night. I said my goodbyes to those in the band who were still talking to me, jumped in the car and headed for home. It had been a tough day, and by the time I hit the freeway I was feeling tired and worn out. I needed to hear some music. I grabbed the first cassette I could find on the passenger seat and banged it into the player. It was the Rolling Stones' *Exile on Main Street*. The first song, 'Rocks Off', filled the car and I put my foot down. I had home in my sights and the wind at my tail. My 6.9-litre Mercedes that was built for the autobahn purred like a cat. 'Tonight,' I thought, 'I might just hit 250 kilometres an hour.'

Five kilometres down the freeway, I looked up and saw, to my horror, that there was another police car on my tail. Its lights were flashing and when I turned down the music I could hear the screaming of its siren. I glanced at the speedo: 225 kilometres an hour. I was in trouble. Should I make a break for it? Surely his puny little police car couldn't keep up with me.

I decided to pull over and throw myself at this cop's mercy. I got out of the car, hoping he'd be a really big music fan.

The police car door opened and he stepped out. As he walked through the glare of his headlights, I recognised something familiar about his gait. Then I saw his face. It was the same cop I'd met earlier that day. He must have been doing a double shift.

'Good evening, Jimmy,' he began. 'Mate, you should really get yourself a four cylinder.'

# *Driving Songs*

| | |
|---|---|
| 'Hit the Road Jack' | RAY CHARLES |
| 'Whole Lotta Shakin' Going On' | JERRY LEE LEWIS |
| 'The Girl Can't Help It' | LITTLE RICHARD |
| 'Shipping Steel' | COLD CHISEL |
| 'Riff Raff' | AC/DC |
| 'Anthem' | THE SENSATIONAL ALEX HARVEY BAND |
| 'Rocks Off' | THE ROLLING STONES |
| 'Maybellene' | CHUCK BERRY |
| 'Hot Rod Lincoln' | CHARLEY RYAN AND THE LIVINGSTON BROS. |
| 'Gimme a Bullet' | AC/DC |
| 'Photograph' | DEF LEPPARD |
| '(Let the) Good Times Roll' | THE CARS |
| 'Rip This Joint' | THE ROLLING STONES |
| 'Six Days on the Road' | DAVE DUDLEY |
| 'Highway to Hell' | AC/DC |
| 'Sweet Little Lisa' | DAVE EDMUNDS |
| 'Willin'' | LITTLE FEAT |

# Across the Tracks

On my most recent trip to Glasgow, we stayed at a nice little boutique hotel we'd found a few years back, not far from where I grew up.

It was tucked away in charming, tree-lined Blythswood Square, just a stone's throw from the very streets we ran wild in as children. I hadn't gone to Glasgow this time to find out anything in particular about my past, I never really do, but something always seems to turn up. Some of the things I have found out have been good, some have been shocking, but they're all pieces of my story that was shattered and scattered by time and trauma. My childhood, for good or bad, seems to come back into focus when I go to Glasgow, and this trip was no different.

The hotel's proximity to our old neighbourhood left me a little bit confused because it was far from anything I'd pictured or remembered – I had no recollection of anything so nice being anywhere near us. I suddenly realised that just by walking a few streets away from our old tenement in what was in my day one of the roughest parts of Glasgow, you could miraculously find yourself in a small but elegant and safe haven.

So I felt at home in the hotel. It was warm and comfortable, but I could walk out its door and stroll down the hill and in fifteen minutes or so find myself surrounded by familiar buildings that once towered over me as a child. Blackened by years of coal fires, some of the three-storey stone tenements that had needed a good clean back in 1960 still stood.

It was while staying in Blythswood Square that I met two new relatives I never knew I had. I was shocked, because since leaving Scotland sixty-four years earlier I'd never heard a word about them, not even a mention of their names. They weren't blood relatives, but, as I'd find out, they had obviously known me well as a small child – in fact, probably as well as anyone I've met from that time.

The meeting came about after I arranged to have dinner with my cousins Joanne and Jackie, and their partners, Jim and Jacqueline, both nights we were in Glasgow. In fact, the only reason we were there this time was to see them. Jane and I had found a restaurant that served top-quality traditional Scottish fare – Joanne doesn't like fancy food and I wanted it to be just right for her. She is the most Glaswegian girl I've ever known. She is absolutely adorable, and she makes me smile whenever I'm near her. Jackie is a quiet-spoken, old-fashioned Glasgow hard man, tough but gentle at the same time.

Reconnecting with my cousins has helped bring joy to my life. Looking at them, I have a picture of what I might have been like if I had stayed in Glasgow. I can tell that the distance has changed me in a lot of ways – twelve thousand miles of separation tends to have that effect. We are very different, but the love we have for each other has survived intact. I get a bit teary just writing about Joanne and Jackie. It must be due to them being the only connection to my old life in Scotland. My cousins don't seem to carry their problems around with them like my side of the family do. In Glasgow you have to get on with life; there seems to be no other way.

Anyway, the first night arrived and Jackie called me on the phone to break some bad news to me. 'Hey, Jim. Our Uncle Archie has surprised us with a visit from Canada and we might have to blow out one of our dinners. He and his wife, Patsy, just landed. I never even knew they were coming. It's a fuckin' pain, but what dae ye do? They're relatives.'

He wasn't happy about it, and Joanne was in tears. But as the Canadians had just arrived that day and they were very old, Jackie could see no other way out. They would have to take them to dinner. At that point I was unaware of any connection to their aunt and uncle, but I was sure if they were their family then, technically, they were 'my ain folk', as the Scots say.

'Why don't we all have dinner together?' I suggested. 'I'll check with the restaurant and make sure we can get a bigger table.'

'Aye, that'd be great, Jimmy. But it's a Friday night and they might be packed at the place, seeing how good it is and aw that, so if they cannae squeeze us in maybe we can catch up fur a wee drink after dinner. These guys are awfie auld and they'll be in bed early. I'm fuckin' sure o' that.'

'Leave it with me, Jackie, and I'll call you back.'

I called the restaurant and, much to my surprise, they told me we could bring as many people as we wanted.

'It's going to be a big gang of us,' I explained hesitantly.

'Och, we don't care, the more the merrier. Bring a football team if you like. It doesnae matter.'

I began to worry. They said on their website that the food was top-notch, yet I could still walk in with a football team on a Friday night and get a table? It might be empty for a good reason, but it was a chance we'd have to take. I told Jackie to bring the relatives along and we headed nervously down to the restaurant.

Archie and Patsy were exactly what I'd expected: quiet and polite at first, just like most of the older Scottish relatives I'd met. Except when Archie spoke to Patsy. When we got to our table, he pulled out a seat for her like an old gentleman and bellowed, 'Aye, there ye go, Patsy. Sit doon here and shut it, okay.' As she sat down, he turned to me and said, 'She's as deef as a post. Just nod and smile at her occasionally and she'll be happy.' Then he walked around the table and sat beside me.

It turned out Archie and Patsy had been close friends of Mum and Dad's, and Archie was the brother of my Uncle Jackie, who was married to my mum's sister, my Aunty Maude, mother of Joanne and Jackie. So technically he was an uncle. Aunty Maude was our closest relative in the world, and I loved her very much. By then, she was our only relative on my mother's side left in Glasgow. Mum's other sisters had moved away as soon as they could – I have a feeling they were running from the same things that my mum was – and we never got the chance to get close to them. Maude, though, stayed in Glasgow with her mother, Betty, my granny. She was a tough Glaswegian woman, and she wasn't leaving her home for anybody or anything. Mum had always made a point of keeping us away from everyone on Dad's side of the family, for reasons that only she understood. But I guessed it was because the families just didn't like each other, and Dad's relatives might have known too much about my mum's dark past.

The menus arrived and I watched as Jane looked for something that she might be able to eat. With no sign of any rice on the menu, I feared she might be in trouble, but she found rope-grown mussels with garlic, horseradish and chilli. In fact, there were lots of interesting dishes on offer, but without a second look my cousins and my new acquaintances all ordered haggis, neeps and tatties served with whisky cream. I ordered Highland venison, trying to look like I was at home with the cuisine.

Drinks were next to be ordered. I opted for an Irn-Bru to keep the Scottish theme going, while Jane and all the others, except for Joanne, immediately asked for whisky. Joanne ordered a wee bottle of lemonade, which I thought was an unusual choice for her, until it arrived and she pulled a bottle of vodka from her bag and half-filled the glass.

'I'm no payin' a fuckin' fortune for drinks fae this place, Jim,' she told me. 'I always bring ma own. This is ma brand and I know what a like.'

Dinner started moving along nicely. The whisky and the vodka loosened tongues and before we knew it we were all laughing out loud and having a great time.

Archie told me that he'd been an aspiring boxer in his day and he'd looked up to my father. My dad had even trained him and they'd boxed on the same Scottish team. As he spoke, Patsy, who was a woman of few words, sat and nodded politely. But later on, as the party loosened up, so did Patsy. At one point, she looked at me across the table and shouted, 'Ye look like yer fuckin' ma. I hope ye didnae get her temper. She was a violent woman was Dot.'

I had to reassure her that I was a pacifist. 'I must have got that from my dad,' I joked.

'Aye, that'd be fuckin' right. He was a bad bastard as well, so he was.' Then she went back to sipping her drink and staring at the wall.

After dinner, we went back to our hotel for 'a few bevvies and a wee chat', as Archie so politely put it. Patsy wanted to go straight home to bed, but I don't think Archie wanted to go down without a fight.

We were sitting there having a few drinks when Patsy got her second wind. As she knocked back her second or third drink, she suddenly confessed to being a good pal of Mum's who had often been in her corner when Mum and Dad went the distance in the ring. Patsy insisted on describing their battles as though they were two prize-fighters and she'd been Mum's trainer.

'Aye, I would cut her eyes so she could see.' She laughed and coughed at the same time, almost choking in the process, then took a minute to breathe before continuing. 'And I'd wave the towel in her face and try to get some fuckin' air into her lungs. It was a waste of time really. She screamed that much at yer dad it was obvious she had plenty of fuckin' oxygen.'

Half the room could hear Patsy talk. Several guests stiffened and curled their lips; others bowed their heads and surreptitiously rolled their eyes at each other. But Patsy didn't notice. And I got the feeling she wouldn't have cared if she had. She and Patsy had been transported back to the late 1950s and they were happy to be there. It was as if the hotel had brought back a flood of memories for the two of them and they were desperate to share them with us. The stories started coming thick and fast.

'I used to push her back out to him so she could kill the bastard, so I fuckin' did. I would have taken a knife tae him if he'd hit me like that.'

Jane and me with my first cousin Joanne Duffy (left) and Jackie's wife, Jacqueline.

It seemed Patsy hadn't been one for throwing in the towel, and Mum just wouldn't stay down.

So, when Archie and Patsy said they were close to Mum and Dad, it now seemed like an understatement. They went on to tell me how they used to hit the town, drink together and kick up their heels on most Saturday nights, and quite a few other nights of the week as well. Archie talked about the trouble he and my dad used to get into. It all sounded cold and frightening to me, but everyone else at the table just laughed about it.

They'd lived on the same street as we did. Their place was in the tenement next door, and whenever Mum and Dad weren't getting on, I would be sent over to Archie and Patsy's house to keep me out of the firing line. My sister Linda was sent to Aunty Maude's house for the same reasons. I still don't think the two of us got off totally unscathed, but these escapes softened the blows that would have been flying constantly. After all, we were the youngest, aside from Alan, who was still a baby, so we needed saving most. God knows what my big brother and sister, who weren't much older than us, had to live through.

It turned out I'd spent a lot of time with Archie and Patsy. Considering how much I recall about Glasgow, I'm surprised that I still don't remember them. Looking into their old faces that night, there was something about them that was comforting, but that was all.

Patsy got a bit misty with the talk of the old days and needed a trip to the bathroom to get some fresh air and gather her thoughts. 'I've got tae go to the toilet before a pee ma fuckin' pants,' she announced.

As she walked by, she touched my cheek and quietly whispered, 'Aye, son, you look just like yer ma.'

I could tell there were more stories to come. While the girls were in the bathroom, Archie, who had been waiting his turn, dying to talk about something, started to blurt out his own recollections from the old days.

'Hey, Jackie, you know this place we're sitting in right now used to be a "gentlemen's club",' he said, making quote marks with his fingers. 'It was dead posh. Aw red velvet and cushions, so it was. Jim's dad and I worked here as security. Fuck, we found some trouble in here. Lucky the walls were already red because they were worse by the time we'd finished. Aye, and we looked after aw the lassies as well. It was great fun. Aye, we even looked after old Betty. After aw, she was one o' the girls too.'

He suddenly turned white, realising that he'd lost control of his tongue and had just told us that my granny had worked in a brothel. He quickly picked up his double whisky from the table and drank it down in one gulp. His eyes dropped to examine the ground.

'Well, it's getting late now, and I'd better take Patsy home before she has another drink and starts trouble,' he mumbled. 'We're awfie auld, you know, and we don't really know what we're talking about anymore. Just talkin' shite. Ye know?'

But his memory was fine and so was Patsy's. They had both painted a finely detailed picture of our lives back in the fifties and early sixties. The life we had run halfway around the world to escape.

Archie stood up awkwardly, rocking slightly on his feet, put on his coat, placed his scarf around his neck and his hat on his head, and reached out his old, wrinkled hand. He was visibly trembling by this point and shook hands with everyone without looking anyone in the face. When he got to me he looked up with a tear in his eye and said, 'It's been lovely to see you again, young Jim. Please send my best to yer mum and dad when you see them.'

I was thinking he might be seeing them before I did.

Patsy came back from the bathroom and seemed surprised that they were leaving – I think she was ready for a big night. She grabbed her coat and kissed my cheek and with that they left. I never had the heart to tell them that their old pals had been gone for a while. It would have made them both too sad.

All in all, it had been an enlightening evening. I'd heard stories about my dad's chequered past that I sort of knew anyway, and some light had been thrown on my granny's unusual choice of jobs – a red light. Until that night, it had been mere hearsay, the kind of stuff that no one talks about. Unless they are well over eighty years old, jet-lagged and full of whisky.

It had been so good to see someone else from way back when. And although Archie might have felt a bit uncomfortable about what came out of his mouth, he had filled in a few blanks that had puzzled me for years, and I was really grateful for that. I would never judge anyone, especially the ones I love and those who had their backs to the wall long before I came along.

Later, I read up on Blythswood Square. The gentlemen's club is mentioned in some articles, but it's talked about like it was a club for old men to sit around in and talk about cars. Eventually I heard that in our day the square was the local red-light area. So that was why we were never allowed to go near it. Just in case we caught someone we knew going to work, I guess.

# The Sacred Heart

Mary searches the drawer in the hallway to find the key that opens the safety lock she had installed on the front door of her apartment a few years back.

Having located it, she turns it in the lock and slowly pulls the door open. Visitors are so rare these days, and the simple act of responding to a knock or a ring of the bell takes time. For years, Mary was security conscious, but now the extra locks are just a nuisance to her. By the time she gets the door open, the delivery boy who rang the bell has gone and is probably halfway back to the store. She was hoping to say hello, maybe have a short conversation, but there's no sign of him. Just her bags of shopping piled up on the step. She sighs softly to herself, then one by one lifts the bags and moves them into the kitchen.

As she places the last bag on the table, her tired eyes rest for a second on the painting on her wall, of Jesus holding a flaming red heart. The frame was once gold and shiny but now looks old and worn. Like her faith, it's a relic from the past and means nothing to her anymore. After her husband passed away ten years ago, she prayed for a companion. Someone she could talk to. Even just a friend. Anyone to take away the constant loneliness that ate at her. But God never heard her. He'd stopped listening to her prayers long ago.

She's still alone, enclosed by walls that once were beautiful but are now damp and mouldy, and covered in marks and stains. Walls that seem to close in on her more and more each day. Her world is shrinking.

She struggles to catch her breath and her tired eyes drift from the picture of the sacred heart to the floor as she walks to the window, stops and stares down at the busy street below. How did life pass her by? She didn't even notice until it was too late. It seems like only yesterday she was young and life was still there in front of her. Now she sits and waits for the end.

Her family stopped visiting months ago. She knows they're too busy doing better, more important things. Increasingly, she feels like a burden to them. They hardly make time to see her at all, and every day she misses them. On the desk, her telephone sits silent. No one has called her. She's not even sure if the phone still works. She lifts the receiver to her ear. The purr of the dial tone sounds like lonely cicadas calling out to others as the last rays of light are swallowed by the darkness. She listens and for a second her mind drifts back to happier times when she'd speak on the phone often. Then she gently places the phone back on the cradle and takes a seat. Everything seems slow and getting slower.

These few musty rooms are all she has now. Too scared to open the door and too frail to manage the stairs, she no longer leaves the apartment. She misses the world outside. But the outside she knew was a different world. Cars move quickly by these days, never stopping. People rush through the busy streets, never talking. All she wants is simple human contact. It's not a lot to ask for. A hello or a nod of the head would be enough to fill the gaping hole in her heart.

From the corner of her eye she senses movement. A single bird, a pigeon, dull and grey, lands on the table on her balcony. She watches as it moves towards the seeds she's set out carefully on a saucer. Every day at the same time, the bird comes seeking food, eats its fill then flies away. If she could fly away like the bird, she would never return to that balcony. She'd fly straight up beyond the buildings, through the haze and the smoke from the factories that blankets the city, beyond the clouds, angry and full of rain, up to where the sky is blue and clear. There she would glide on the wind, and never come down again.

Her thoughts draw her outside. Leaving the room, she forgets her pain for a moment and manages to climb onto the chair by the railing. She looks down at the street below. All at once, her eyes feel sharper than they've been for a long, long time, and the future is crystal clear.

There's no more looking back. It's time to spread her wings.

# The Texas Tornado Jam

The Cold Chisel tour of America in 1981 was a real trial. The American music scene wasn't ready for us, and, more importantly, we weren't ready for the American music scene.

We had worked for years in Australia to get to a place where we were in control of our direction and the music we wanted to play, and I guess we had become big fish in a small pond. Suddenly we were back to being very small fish in a very big pond, and no one cared about what we wanted or what we were trying to do. We were sent on tour with a few bands we couldn't relate to, playing to audiences who didn't know us, and by the time we got to Texas, only a couple of shows into the tour, we were fed up and almost ready to go home.

Texas, though, was a breath of fresh air. It was a place where the music scene was organic and earthy. Bands played with heart and soul, and not everything was about being the next big thing. Texas reminded us a lot of Australia in the seventies. It was wild and the Texans we met, like us, didn't think that Los Angeles was the centre of the universe. We could relax and just play rock 'n' roll.

Many of the bands that came from Texas sounded like they could survive playing the pubs in Australia. They were gritty, blues-based and soulful. Bands like Edgar and Johnny Winter, ZZ Top and The Fabulous Thunderbirds. These were bands I'd grown up listening to – in fact there was a record by Edgar Winter's band White Trash called *Roadwork* that had changed the way I sang forever. A double live album, it featured Edgar and Johnny Winter and a singer named Jerry LaCroix, and I played it every day for about two years. It's the record that taught me to scream.

The bus driver told us he used to drive for Elvis. But I think every bus driver in America gave us that story. *(Rod Willis)*

So the one event on the tour we'd been looking forward to was the South Texas Tornado Jam in Austin, Texas, on 11 July. The first Tornado Jam had been set up in 1980 by musician Joe Ely in his hometown of Lubbock, to honour fellow citizen Buddy Holly and mark the day in 1970 when tornadoes had devastated the town. The following year's South Texas Tornado Jam, at Manor Downs, just outside Austin, was arranged partly to raise money for victims of recent flooding. Booked on the bill with us were The Fabulous Thunderbirds, Stevie Ray Vaughan, Al Kooper, Delbert McClinton and the Joe Ely Band.

As the day approached, we were champing at the bit to get on stage with all these great bands, and it didn't even matter to us that we had to play early. There was a good chance that it would feel like a late-night gig to me anyway, as I'd spent a lot of time on that tour not sleeping and becoming increasingly wound up. I remember being ready to kill by the time we got to the venue.

There were a few bands on before us, but by the time we arrived we had missed them and we were almost immediately rushed towards the stage by the production manager, which was probably a good thing as we didn't have time to feel nervous. The production manager was a whisky-swilling, God-fearing, tattooed good old boy with a hat as big as his heart. Now I think about it, we were probably the only people at the whole show not wearing cowboy hats, so we must have been easy to spot.

As we made our way through the backstage area, I noticed that a lot of the other bands appeared to be friends, and they were all milling around, eating, drinking beer and generally getting themselves pumped up and ready to play. I knew I wanted to make an impression on these guys.

We were a fierce band by this time, and we hit the first song like it was our last and kept going up from there. 'Conversations' doesn't particularly sound like a Texan song, but the crowd lit up as soon as we started it. Ian was on fire, the rhythm section was pumping, Don was playing piano like Jerry Lee Lewis on amphetamines, and me, well, I was just doing what I did every night.

We didn't talk a lot between songs. I figured that no one would understand a word I said anyway, so we just tore from one song to the next. 'Khe Sanh' rolled right into 'Rising Sun', at which point we stopped just long enough to drink anything we could get our hands on before playing 'Houndog' and telling the audience what it was like travelling up and down the east coast of Australia. The set steadily gained momentum and with every song the band seemed to get heavier and heavier. I could see some members of the other bands gathering at the side of stage and scratching their heads, as if they were thinking, 'What the hell have these boys been taking?'

'My Baby', 'Star Hotel' and 'Merry-Go-Round' had the band whipping up a sweat. We were firing on all cylinders. Then we slowed things down with 'One Long Day', though I realised later that our slow song was faster than most of the other bands' up-tempo songs. While Ian sang, I paced around the stage, drinking vodka and waiting to jump back in. 'Standing on the Outside' started up, and I felt pretty sure they didn't make songs like that around there.

The side of stage was getting busy. 'Goodbye' was our last song and it was like an out-of-control freight train heading for Austin railway station. Ian was playing blistering guitar, Don was banging the keys and I was screaming like a banshee for the whole song. We crashed into a deafening finish, walked off and headed for the stairs to leave the stage.

But the production manager cut us off. 'Hell, where do you think you boys are going? You'd better be playing another song or someone might get themselves killed.'

We walked back on and started 'Wild Thing'. Just the guitar at first, then when we'd all settled in we hit them right between the eyes. After the first verse the stage felt too small for me, and I was looking for some new territory to prowl. I've recounted what happened next elsewhere, but it's a story that bears repeating.

I decided to climb the scaffolding that supported the loudspeakers. I was about twenty feet in the air when I was finally ready to sing the next verse. Preparing to scream,

I sucked in the biggest breath I could take – I wanted this to be loud.

As I did so, a huge Texan moth – yes, they do grow things bigger there – flew into my mouth. I nearly swallowed it – if I had, it would have been the first thing I'd eaten all week – but I choked on it, then spat the beast down towards the ground. Unfortunately, our tour manager, Mark Pope, was following me up the scaffolding, feeding my microphone cable to me, and the moth and a large mouthful of A-grade Russian moonshine landed on his head. He wobbled and nearly fell.

Now, I've had people scream at me while I'm performing, throw beer, even bottles, at me; I've been punched, thrown from the stage. But the Texan moth incident was one of my most shocking on-stage experiences, and one that nearly ruined the day. Fortunately, I managed to steady myself and recover. But there were more challenges to come.

As Ian's guitar solo raged, I continued to the very top of the scaffolding and looked down on the stage. From there I could see half of the county, which was wide and flat. All the other musicians were standing with their mouths open, wondering how I was going to get back down. That thought didn't cross my mind until the guitar solo was nearly over. I scrambled down a few feet and realised that at that rate I wouldn't make it down in time to start the next verse. I had no choice but to jump.

You'd be amazed how athletic I can be on a fuel of clear spirits and moths. I sailed through the air, feeling like I was in slow motion, as the crowd stared silently. *Bang!* I hit the stage just as I had to start singing. My timing was perfect and the crowd went wild. After that, I tore the stage to pieces, Ian kicked over his amps and we walked off. We'd been more like a tornado than a band, and I figured that's what they'd wanted.

'That was fun,' I said to the rest of the band as we pushed our way past the other performers. 'We'll have to come back here. I think they liked us.'

We certainly made a lot of good friends that day, in the crowd and backstage. Later I jumped up to sing with Stevie Ray Vaughan and his brother Jimmie, as well as a bunch of other great singers, including Delbert McClinton and Joe Ely.

Many years later Jimmie Vaughan toured Australia with his band The Fabulous Thunderbirds and we caught up. Jimmie was a slow-moving, blues-guitar-playing cowboy and he came out to somewhere in western Sydney to jam with my band. I guess he thought being out west he would fit right in. But we were playing in Blacktown or somewhere like that and the music we were playing was as far from western swing as you could get. I remember looking over and seeing him playing guitar faster than he'd probably ever played before and breaking out in a

Me on stage with Joe Ely and his band. *(Rod Willis)*

sweat as he tried to keep up. We laughed about it later as we recalled my first visit to Texas.

Joe Ely became a very close friend of ours and we later brought him out to Australia to tour with us. I remember stopping on a drive somewhere up the east coast with Joe on a cold, clear, cloudless night and Joe being amazed as he gazed up at the stars. 'Hell, Jimmy, we have these same stars at home in Texas, but they've all been turned around somehow. I feel like I'm standing on my head down here. It sure is pretty though.' Despite being upside down, Joe clearly felt as much at home with us in Australia as we did when we went to Texas.

There was also a little guy who joined us on stage at the Tornado Jam, playing guitar, and who was only about twelve years old at the time. I figured he might have been a bit overwhelmed by the whole thing, so I leaned in to encourage him. But it turned out he didn't need my help. Charlie Sexton was a monster even back then. He went on to play guitar for David Bowie and Bob Dylan, and he even came out and played in my band for a while. Since that day he has been like one of our kids: whenever he comes to Australia, we catch up and watch him play.

I must get back to Texas some time soon. At a time in my life when I felt I didn't fit in anywhere, that was the one place where I was really at home.

# Texas Tornadoes

| | |
|---:|:---|
| 'The House Is Rockin'' | STEVIE RAY VAUGHAN |
| 'Tuff Enuff' | THE FABULOUS THUNDERBIRDS |
| 'Take Me to the River' | DELBERT McCLINTON |
| 'Dallas' | JOE ELY |
| 'Wild Thing' | COLD CHISEL |
| 'Beat's So Lonely' | CHARLIE SEXTON |
| 'Jesus Just Left Chicago' | ZZ TOP |
| 'Be Careful with a Fool' | JOHNNY WINTER |
| 'Conversations' | COLD CHISEL |
| 'Frankenstein' | THE EDGAR WINTER GROUP |
| 'Rock and Roll, Hoochie Koo' | RICK DERRINGER |
| 'Lookin' for a Home' | AL KOOPER AND SHUGGIE OTIS |
| 'Six Strings Down' | JIMMIE VAUGHAN |
| 'One Long Day' (*Swingshift* version) | COLD CHISEL |
| *Roadwork* (whole album) | EDGAR WINTER'S WHITE TRASH |

# Staph Party

As I get older, I seem to be spending more and more time in hospital. Not out of choice but out of necessity, and much to my dismay.

Just before Christmas 2022, much to my horror (and as I've recounted elsewhere), I had to have a hip replacement. I then spent the first half of 2023 doing physio, convalescing in Thailand and trying to get myself back on stage. By the second half of the year, I was feeling better than I had in years: I was lean, fit and in top singing form. So I rescheduled a bunch of shows I'd had to cancel the year before and got ready to hit the road. Only to find myself almost immediately falling apart again.

The warning signs came in November, which was a very busy month for me. As well as the shows, I had books to write and huge anniversary parties to sing at, and, to top it all off, at the end of the month I was due to play two gigs on a cruise ship sailing from Noumea to Sydney, full of wild people who wanted to go crazy. In fact, that last week of November was shaping up to be the busiest week of my career.

The week began in Melbourne, where I was booked to be filmed singing five songs at the ABC for a Christmas special. I know what you're saying: 'Five songs is nothing, Jimmy. You could sing five songs with one lung tied behind your back.' Yeah, normally I could, even taking into consideration that when you're filming you need to rehearse the songs about five times for the sound people, five times for the lighting operators and then a few more times for the cameras. So singing five songs turns into singing fifty or more songs in one afternoon. Still pretty easy for me, though, right?

Wrong. In the days leading up to that intense week I hadn't been feeling my usual chirpy self. I was still swimming every day and doing Pilates every second day, but, truth be known, I felt like shit. It wasn't like I hadn't felt that way before – I've done whole tours feeling like I wasn't firing on all cylinders. But normally when this happened it was self-inflicted and I just had to lift my game. This time, though, nothing seemed to help me get happening. I had vitamin shots, I drank green juices, and I was getting a lot of rest – you name it, I tried it.

I managed to get through the days filming at the ABC, although reviewing the footage now I don't look so well. As soon as I finished, I got into bed, to give myself a chance of recovering and fulfilling my obligations. But the next morning I felt terrible: I had a fever and a cough and a backache to boot. The show had to go on though, so we jumped on a charter flight out of Melbourne to Mildura, on the Murray River near the South Australia–Victoria border.

By the time I got to the venue, I thought I was going to pass out. I drank lots of cold water in an attempt to bring my temperature down. It didn't work. As showtime drew near, I gargled with honey, hot water and cider vinegar to help me sing, but nothing I did made me feel fit enough to do the show. I had an excruciating pain in my back, and the longer I waited to go on, the worse it got. The Living End were playing right before us and, as usual, they were amazing – they play loud, hard and fast. I had no idea how I could possibly follow them. But it's my job, so I hit the stage.

That performance is all a bit of a blur now, but apparently we did a killer show. Then it was back on the plane to Melbourne to get ready for Mushroom's fiftieth anniversary concert at the Rod Laver Arena. I was opening the show at around 6.45 pm, and it was to be broadcast nationally on Channel Seven. Jane helped me into bed as soon as we walked in the hotel door, and I went straight to sleep. But, overnight, things got much worse. The following morning Jane had to ask a doctor to come to the hotel and give me a vitamin shot. I knew then I was in big trouble.

The band and myself had to be at the arena to do a final sound and camera check before they opened the doors; luckily we had managed to do most of the checks the previous day before going to Mildura. By now I felt like I was dying. My fever had gone through the roof and the pain had gone way beyond being bearable. I had to fill myself with painkillers for the pain and aspirin for the fever if I was going to have any chance of doing the show.

We got to the stage on time and played two songs, both ridiculously high to sing and both needing all the energy

I could muster. I don't really remember the show at all; I've seen it since and I look like a corpse. Straight from the stage, we were rushed to the airport to catch a plane back to Sydney. We had a flight to Noumea at six the next morning. Somehow they got us onto the Sydney flight and then I was back home in Botany. But I couldn't get out of bed for the flight to Noumea. I couldn't even stand up.

By lunchtime I was in hospital in Sydney, and I was critical. Over the next few days I drifted in and out of consciousness. The doctors gave me drugs for the pain and drugs for the fever, but the main thing they needed to do was get to the bottom of what was happening to me. There's a blood test that shows infection markers in your blood. The normal reading is under five. By the time I reached hospital, mine was somewhere around 410. I wasn't sure what that meant, but I knew it wasn't good.

I seemed to be constantly surrounded by specialists and each time I opened my eyes a new one had joined the group. In the end there were seven of the best doctors in Sydney working on me. First I was diagnosed with bacterial pneumonia. They treated that with antibiotics, and after a few days the markers came down, but only to 395. I was still in danger.

Soon I'd had every test known to medicine. Blood tests and blood cultures, MRIs, CAT scans, X-rays, angiograms, echocardiograms and other ultrasounds, but still they couldn't find the problem. Finally, my neurologist insisted on an MRI with contrast – a dye that's injected into your veins so that your organs and tissues can be seen more clearly. When he came back with the results, I knew he'd found something.

A staph infection, he said. *Staphylococcus aureus* had settled in my back. And that had resulted in sepsis, an extremely dangerous condition where the body's defences against infection start to turn on its organs and tissues. The reason the staph was in my back was that the bug goes to places in your body where there is little or no blood flow, and my back had a lot of scar tissue from a series of surgeries I'd had there about nine years earlier.

A decision was made to operate, and next day I went in for back surgery. The surgeons found an abscess near my spine that was infected and pressing on nerves – that's why I couldn't walk. They drained a lot of pus and other revolting muck, cleaned the area with antiseptics and what not, stitched me back up and pumped me full of antibiotics, hoping it would kill any remaining staph in the area.

More blood tests followed and, disappointingly, my infection markers didn't go down that much: they were sitting somewhere in the low two hundreds. The staph bug was still in my body, and the doctors urgently needed to find it and kill it. There were two places where they were most worried it might settle. The more serious one was my heart, and I was particularly vulnerable because I'd had my aortic valve replaced sixteen years earlier with an artificial bovine and plastic valve. There was a chance I might end up needing a new valve.

The 'less serious' location was my new hip joint. That would mean surgery to drain and clean all the staph from my hip. Then I would have to wear a drainage bag for three months or more to make sure it was all gone, before having the hip replacement redone – an operation that essentially involves sawing your leg off and reattaching it. Great. The best-case scenario was I'd be out of action for twelve months.

More tests followed, and it seemed that every time I went for one, the predominantly Irish nurses who were working on me – for some reason there were a lot of very good Irish nurses working in that hospital – were all getting ready for their Christmas break. As I lay in the MRI machine while it was being operated by young nurses with tinsel in their hair and Christmas decorations hanging off the equipment, we chatted and they told me about the upcoming staff Christmas party.

'Surely, you guys could take me to the party with you,' I joked.

'No, Jimmy. I'm sorry, it's for staff only.'

'Well, I've got staph,' I quipped. 'Does that not count?'

'We'll have to look into that,' one of the nurses replied. 'You might just meet the right criteria to get a ticket. And

I'm sure we could get you one if you would sing. But the problem is that you can't even stand up, Jimmy, never mind sing and dance.'

I'm sure if I could have walked they would have taken me, but it looked like I was going to be stuck in hospital over Christmas and would have to have my own party. One for people with staph infections. That would be a cheerful group, wouldn't it?

After fifteen days, my markers were still sky high. Luckily, so was I: they kept pumping me full of painkillers after the back surgery. As good as being high as a kite and lying in bed sounds, the drugs were not my drugs of choice. At this stage of my life I was happy being drug free, and the painkillers were making me feel sick. I wanted out of there, but Camilla Wainwright, my cardiologist, being extremely thorough, wasn't having a bar of it. 'Look, let's wait a few more days, Jimmy. I'm sure the bug will show up, and you don't want that to happen if we're not around.'

Begrudgingly, I agreed to stay put. While I wanted to be in my own bed in my own house, I knew that I was too sick to go anywhere. At this point Camilla ordered another test, a PET (positron emission tomography) scan. This involves injecting the patient with a mildly radioactive substance so that the doctors can monitor processes across the whole body. If there is any infection or growth, this test will find it. I was a little worried about having a

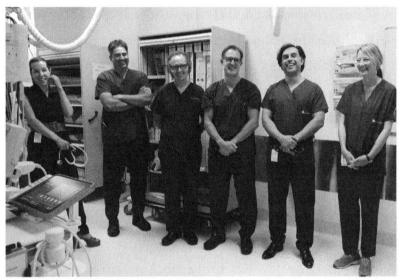
This is some of the A team who saved my life. From left to right: Doctors Orley Lavee, Paul Jansz, John Rooney, Mark Winder, Scott Chapman and Camilla Wainwright. *(courtesy of the Nine Network)*

radioactive substance injected into me but figured I'd done worse to myself on a Saturday night back in the old days in search of a good time.

I lay in bed as we waited anxiously for the results.

'Honest, I think I'm feeling better,' I said to Jane.

'You look like a ghost, Jimmy. You're not better. Let's just wait and see.'

Camilla came back with the results and as soon as she walked into the room I knew just by looking at her that it wasn't good news. The infection had gone to my heart and they could see it on my aortic valve. I'd always known that valve might need to be replaced at some point, as had the surgeons, who'd given me one that was big enough to be replaced laparoscopically – by inserting a smaller replacement valve inside the old one, via the main artery running up from my thigh. That didn't sound too bad. Relatively.

But when my new heart surgeon, Paul Jansz, took a look at the results, he decided he would have to do open-heart surgery. What's more, he wouldn't know exactly what was required until he opened up my chest. It was all out of my hands, and the operation had to be done immediately or I might die. It was lunchtime when Paul told me this, and by nine o'clock the next morning I was in theatre again.

By now it was like I was on a first-name basis with all the anaesthetists.

'Morning, Frank.'

'Morning, Jimmy. What are you having today?'

'Open-heart.'

'Right, that's good. Did you watch the Tigers game last night? They were terrible.'

'No, missed that. I was out of my mind on painkillers.'

'Okay, let's knock you out cold then.'

Well, maybe it wasn't quite like that, but I thought I recognised a lot of the faces. Though in their scrubs, masks and so on they all look alike, so maybe I'd never met any of them before.

Anyway, at that point my world went blank. Jane thought that the operation would take about four hours, so she sat by the phone waiting for news. None came, and five hours ticked by. Still no word. After six hours, Jane called the hospital. She was told that the operation had been very complicated and they had only just finished. I was still on the table with my chest peeled open like a can of sardines. The doctors wanted me to stay that way for an hour in case I didn't stop bleeding, rather than have to open me up again.

Some time that evening, I pulled my eyes open and found myself surrounded by machines and nurses. I was afraid; then I saw my Jane and felt better. The staph infection had not only taken hold on my aortic valve but had also damaged twelve centimetres of my aorta, as well as my mitral valve and the annulus. The whole procedure had been more complicated than a heart transplant, and taken more than six hours.

During that time I felt nothing. There was no light to head towards, and no relatives waiting to escort me to the next world. Maybe because it wasn't my time. When that happens, I hope my little schnauzers, Ollie and Snoop, are there waiting for me. That would be nice, and I'd feel okay about moving on. And then I'd go and get the place set up and looking beautiful for when Jane comes.

# Last Man Standing

Back in the late 1980s, after I'd left Cold Chisel and started my solo career, it seemed that nothing succeeded like excess.

Everything was turned up to eleven – the music, the touring, the drinking – and everything seemed to happen at top speed. It was hard for me to slow down.

It was around this time that we moved to the New South Wales Southern Highlands and bought a place we named The White House, not far from the town of Bowral. Jane had decided we needed to escape the craziness of the city, find some peace and create a beautiful place to raise our children. The house perched on top of Mount Gibraltar, known to locals as 'The Gib'. It's an extinct volcano, and at the end of our street there was a circular clearing, known as 'The Bowl', which was the original crater. Mount Gibraltar isn't very high – just 863 metres above sea level. Like a lot of the mountains in Australia, it probably once reached for the sky, but we live in an ancient continent, and, over millions of years, wind and rain have worn down the landscapes until even what might have been our most imposing mountains now look, just as Mount Gibraltar does, like low hills.

It's a beautiful part of the world, and there is definitely something magical about The Gib. A little bit of its magic even rubbed off on me. I loved getting out early and walking in the morning air, often misty and so silent that I would imagine I was the first person to discover these paths. But I still found it hard to relax completely and was always on the go – and always on edge. I even worried that, although it was many millions of years since The Gib had last blown its top, it was possibly just dormant and, like me, might one day explode, raining fire and terror on everyone around it.

To distract myself and use up some of my nervous energy, I'd ride my horse up and down the many trails that led in and out of The Bowl, pretending I was a cowboy in one of the westerns I used to watch as a child. But even cowboys get hungry, so when it was time to eat I'd turn for home on my trusty steed, thunder up the hill and down my street, charge through our gate, come to a screaming halt outside the stables, leap from the saddle before the horse had even stopped, land on my feet, run to the house and start ransacking the kitchen for food.

My manic behaviour went on for a few years, but then one day, reaching the end of her tether, Jane suggested that I should maybe learn to meditate. When I say *suggested*, I mean she *pleaded* with me to try it.

I couldn't see why someone as unruffled, equable, relaxed, well balanced and calm as me would really need to meditate at all, but then, I thought, 'What do I have to lose?' I also thought it might be good for Jane, as clearly something in her life was stressing her out.

So one lunchtime we all jumped in the car and set out for the Sunnataram Forest Monastery, near the village of Bundanoon, which had been set up by a group of monks from Thailand.

I remember driving out that day, listening to AC/DC on the CD player, and thinking, 'Yes. It'll be nice to sit and be still for a minute or two.'

It was freezing cold when we arrived, but luckily I'd worn my leather jacket. Jane and I walked across the car park and were met by a small man dressed in orange robes, who turned out to be the abbot of the monastery, Pra Manna. He had one of the kindest faces I had ever seen, and peacefulness seemed to ooze out of him. Even I felt surprisingly calm as soon as I stood near him.

We went inside to the temple, where we joined a few other people and Pra Manna asked us all to sit while he gave us a little talk. I looked around. There were no chairs. As everyone else quietly got down on the floor, I realised I was the last man standing. So I slowly and carefully squatted down and tried to tuck my legs under my body and kneel on the ground. That didn't work. I untangled myself and tried to sit cross-legged, something I had not attempted since I was in Grade Two. That didn't work either. Everyone else sat patiently as I puffed and moaned and groaned, trying unsuccessfully to find a position I could bend my legs into that would not cut off the circulation to the rest of my body and end in death.

Finally, a young monk stood up and walked to the next room. A moment later he came back carrying a chair, placed it next to me and gestured for me to sit on it. I slowly pulled my legs out of a knot and tried to stand. I was numb from the waist down, but I managed to drag myself to the chair and collapse onto it.

The room was so quiet. Too quiet: with my leather jacket rustling and squeaking, I could hear every uncomfortable move I was making. How come, I wondered, no one else was moving?

Pra Manna began his talk, providing encouragement for the practice we were about to commence. Suddenly everything he said seemed to be directed at me. He wanted to put into perspective the many challenges I would face while meditating, so that I understood that what I was about to do during the next hour or so would not be easy.

I immediately thought to myself, 'You mean I have to do this for an hour!'

Pra Manna continued, explaining that the talk would help show me the correct path, and that I would experience a feeling of satisfaction and maybe even start to see my true calling in life.

This was all well and good, but did it really need to take an hour?

'I want you all to get comfortable and breathe deeply,' Pra Manna said.

'Thank God for this chair.' I wasn't sure if I had just thought that or spoken it out loud. Fortunately, no one said a word. I'd got away with it.

I closed my eyes and breathed deeply. Or was that a yawn?

I opened one eye and looked around the room to see if anybody had noticed. All good. They seemed to be sound asleep.

'Breathe in through your nose and then breathe out,' Pra Manna instructed.

'God, now my nose is blocked,' I thought. 'I'd better just use my mouth. It'll be noisy, though.'

'Clear your mind. If a thought comes, just acknowledge it and let it go.'

'Got it,' I told myself. 'That one's gone. Oops, it's back. Let it go, Jimmy. Shit, it won't go. What do I do now? Ah, there's another one. Let it go. Okay, I got it. Damn, the first thought is back again.'

This went on for the rest of the hour. Throughout that time, my leather jacket squeaked and creaked and cracked and groaned. And when I eventually decided I'd better take it off, it sounded like I was wrestling an alligator. Mortified, I sat down again and tried to be quiet, but for some strange reason I started to shuffle my feet and kept shifting in my seat. You'd be surprised how noisy shifting in your seat can be.

Then my stomach started to rumble, and I immediately wished I'd eaten just before our visit. It was only a quiet rumble at first, but as the time dragged on it became louder and louder, until deep gurgling noises were echoing around the room.

I carefully opened one eye again, just the tiniest fraction so that I could peer through my eyelashes without anyone noticing. No one else had moved an inch. I quickly closed my eye again and prayed for it all to end.

*Bong!* A small temple bell sounded, and the ringing carried softly across the room, gently bringing the members of the group back to the present. People slowly stretched their hands towards the roof, rubbed their eyes and smiled at each other. I was already standing in my jacket by the door, jiggling my car keys and wondering where I'd left my shoes.

My first trip to the monastery had been eventful. Although I'd felt out of place, even uncomfortable at times, I'd caught a glimpse of something else – a feeling I didn't think I'd ever really felt before, a feeling of peace. Beneath my jittering façade, I knew I'd have to come back. And perhaps if I did, maybe my own volatile core might start to settle and cool, my regular eruptions of anger become fewer and further between. Maybe, like that old volcano, I could chill out, stay quiet and calm – for a while at least.

# The Swarm

Although Theodore Scott had been retired for over six months, he was still struggling with the transition from office work to a so-called life of leisure.

Up until now it hadn't gone well. In fact, it had left him feeling empty. It was as if his life and his world had been turned upside down. Unless he was in the garden tending his roses, he found himself out of sorts and annoyed by the smallest of things. He seemed to spend half his day getting himself into a state of high anxiety and then the other half trying, unsuccessfully, to get himself out of that state.

In his job at the accounting firm he'd felt he had a purpose. He could go to the office in the morning, sit down at his desk and work without being bothered until the end of the day, when the boss looked at his watch and told him it was time to go home. Not only that, everything he needed was right there on his desk – his pens, his papers, his calculator – and always exactly where he'd left them.

Now his life was a shambles. He had gone from being Theodore, the head of the department who was renowned for working like a well-oiled machine, to just plain old Ted who had practically nothing to do.

Ted was not a name he particularly appreciated, but his wife, Janet, had taken a liking to it. She considered it a term of endearment, thought it sounded nicer and less formal than Theodore, and said that, besides, it was cute. He shivered at the idea of being thought of as cute.

Discontented and mumbling to himself, he walked into the kitchen, stopped at a dresser and opened a drawer to retrieve the keys he'd left there only the night before. As the drawer slid open, a potato moth that had been trapped overnight took flight, fluttering past his face in search of freedom. Startled, he jumped back from the cabinet, knocking over one of his wife's best teacups. It shattered on the floor.

'Ted, what was that?' Janet called from the living room.

He stopped and drew a deep breath before answering. 'Nothing, dear.'

Why was everything so difficult these days? And what was the point of his life now? He knew he was too old to be at work, but it would be better than just pottering around at home and performing house-sitting duties. That was all he was doing currently, looking after his wife's best friend Martha's house while she travelled around Europe with groups of people she didn't know, going to museums all day and dining on weird dishes he'd never heard of. He couldn't think of anything worse.

And now, of course, Martha's keys did not seem to be where he'd left them. Item by item, he meticulously removed everything from the drawer until it was completely empty. No sign of the keys. Barely controlling his frustration, he shouted, 'Janet, have you moved Martha's keys. I put them in the top drawer yesterday and now they're gone. I always put them in the same place. Right at the front of the drawer where I can easily find them.'

'Calm down, Ted,' she replied. 'Yes, I did move them. I hung them on the hook by the stove, where all the other keys are kept.'

He rolled his eyes. Janet hated it when he did that, but she was well out of sight.

He walked across the room towards the stove, stopping for a moment to admire the flowers Janet had picked that morning in the garden. They were lovely – well, of course they were, they were from *his* garden, the one place that brought him pleasure.

Just at that moment, he spotted a bee clambering through the petals of one of the flowers, a Julia's rose, in search of pollen. For an instant, he was startled, but then his pulse slowed and, calmly and with great care, he picked up the vase and moved cautiously towards the door.

'What are you doing with my flowers?' Janet's voice surprised him as she entered the room.

He turned towards her, and the bee flew from the flowers and began circling the table. Its buzzing grew louder as it became more agitated.

'Quick, open the door,' cried Janet, panicking.

Ted remained uncharacteristically calm. Bees didn't worry him, it seemed. Well, he had heard they would only sting you if you were afraid.

He strolled over to the door and opened it. Sunshine poured into the room, and the bee, sensing freedom, flew straight towards the light and into the garden.

'It must be a good time for them to gather pollen or something,' said Janet. 'There were so many of them in the garden today and I was certain I would be attacked.'

'I can assure you, Janet, they're not going to attack you. The last thing they want to do is sting you.' Ted wasn't sure why he felt so certain about this, but he did.

A moment later, though, he was feeling on edge again. 'Look, I'd better get over to Martha's place to feed her chickens. I promised her I'd look after them while she was gone, you know.' He headed for the door.

'Are you in a hurry to get out of here?' Janet asked as she moved towards the stove.

'Well, I have things to do.'

'Slow down, would you. Just sit down at the table and have your breakfast, and then you can go to Martha's. The chickens will still be there.'

'But Martha told me they need to be fed at nine in the morning and not a minute later.'

'Sit down and eat!' Her tone softened. 'The chickens will survive until nine fifteen. Trust me. Look, I've made your favourite, an egg and bacon sandwich on that lovely fresh white bread I got from the shop this morning.'

She placed the sandwich on the table and smiled at him. 'Come on, Ted, sit down for a minute and spend a bit of time with me.'

How could he refuse? He sheepishly sat down, picked up his sandwich and took a bite. He'd been up since sunrise, had forgotten to eat and was hungrier than he'd realised. That seemed to happen a lot these days. Food just wasn't as important to him as it had once been.

Janet watched him with a look of concern on her face. 'I have to tell you, you're going to be the death of me, Ted.' She sighed as she gently placed a glass of cold water in front of him. 'I don't mind if you run around like a crazy man outside the house, but I wish you could be calm in your own home. Why can't you sit still and watch television or read a book? You're always on the go.'

Ted paused, with the half-finished sandwich falling apart in his hand, watching Janet as she moved silently around the kitchen, and waiting for her blessing so he could get on with his day.

Janet grabbed the broom to clean up the broken cup, sighed and nodded at him.

He jumped up, washed his hands and grabbed the car keys from the hook, kissed her on the head and ran out the door.

The air was crisp and clean, and the sounds of the birds welcoming the morning were almost drowned out by the buzzing of the bees as they moved from flower to flower, busy at their work in the garden. When you're as unsure of your place in the world as Ted usually was, life tends to be a bit of a blur and it's easy to miss the finer details. But, somehow, not today. Now he was outside, he felt more peaceful than he'd felt in a long time. He took a deep breath, closed his eyes and lifted his face to the sun. Something good was surely going to happen; he could feel it.

Resting on their beds nearby, Ted's two best friends, his dogs Yin and Yang, lay waiting for him. He'd rescued them from the pound many years back. They had been there quite a while and seemed to have no prospect of finding a new owner any time soon. But he'd decided the moment he first saw them that, even though they weren't pedigree show dogs or the prettiest dogs in the world, he was taking them home. From then on they followed Ted everywhere he went. He didn't need to say a word; if he was on the move, so were they. They'd jump up and pad softly behind him.

But this morning they just looked up at Ted and wagged their tails, as if they knew something unusual was happening. Ted peered at them, slightly puzzled, then gently said, 'Okay, you guys stay here. In any case, I don't want you to chase Martha's chickens out of the yard again. It took me hours to round them up last time you did that.'

The dogs looked at him with understanding eyes, then got up, walked to the end of the driveway, flopped down on the warm sandstone and lay in the sun.

Ted jumped into his run-down Toyota Corolla hatchback, adjusted the seat and wound the window down to let the cool morning air fill the car. He sat for a moment before starting the engine. Then he shifted the car into gear and backed out of the carport, moving slowly and cautiously, making sure he didn't disturb his two friends, who seemed to be already asleep again in the morning sun.

As he drove out of the garden and turned onto the dirt road, he felt his usual anxiety rising up inside him. He put his foot down on the accelerator and sped off along the dry dirt road.

He had hardly passed the end of his fence line when something out of the ordinary caught his eye. He hit the brakes and came to a sudden stop. A cloud of white dust enveloped the car. As it cleared, he saw the most astonishing sight. In the big gum tree growing between the fence and the road was a huge swarm of bees, hanging from one of the lower branches just inside his fence. It looked like a moving, buzzing, vibrating ball of energy. Just for a second, he panicked and reached for the handle to wind up the window, but the feeling passed and a deep sense of serenity came over him.

He sat for about ten minutes with all the windows of the car wound down, staring at the tree and listening to the hum that emanated from the swarm. Some of the bees from a neighbour's hive must have decided to take the old queen and go in search of a new home. A mass migration – he'd read in one of Janet's books that this sometimes happened in spring. As the realisation that a wild swarm of thousands of bees was right there in a tree on his own property began to sink in, he took a deep breath. As he breathed out, he was sure he heard the hum of the bees become lower and softer.

There was something about this swarm that he liked. Again, surprisingly, he wasn't afraid. Should he have been? He remembered being stung as a child, and that it wasn't much fun. But back then bees had seemed bad-tempered and untrusting, while these ones were clearly more at ease with their surroundings, and with him.

Reassured, he stepped quietly out of the car and moved towards the swarm. The humming of the horde sounded even more soothing, and as he neared it he was sure that the tone softened and the pitch lowered again, to a gentle purring sound. It was as if the bees, unthreatened by his presence, were inviting him to move closer.

He inched forward. One or two of the bees buzzed past his ears without touching him. Were they checking him out? Another scouting party landed on his arm. Woah, what was going on? Surely this was not normal? Very slowly, he raised his arm. As he peered closely at the bees, they took off and flew back to the buzzing mass.

It was crazy, and he needed to think about what was happening, so he slowly moved away and, without making any noise or sudden movements, got back into his car.

He sat alone in the driver's seat, contemplating what had just taken place. He had a strong sense that the bees were happy to have him around. They seemed to know that he wouldn't hurt them, and they appeared to mean him no harm either.

For years he'd thought that he could communicate with the dogs without speaking, but this was a swarm of wild bees. Surely there was no way they could know what he was thinking?

Then he remembered overhearing something about bee charmers one night when Janet was watching a nature channel on TV. He'd assumed it was some sort of magic trick. Yet these bees genuinely seemed to have taken a liking to him. Perhaps he really had that power? 'Maybe I'm a bee charmer,' he told himself.

Still pondering these notions, he started the car, turned and headed back up the driveway, pulled up at the house and walked past the sleeping dogs to the kitchen. He decided it was best not to mention getting so close to the bees to Janet, since she already thought he was as mad as a cut snake, so he simply said, 'Janet, you won't believe it. There's a swarm of bees on our property.'

Janet, in her usual fashion, was entirely underwhelmed by this revelation. She looked up and said, 'That's nice, dear. Somebody should catch them.'

He thought carefully about what he was going to say next. 'Yeah, good idea.'

'Why don't you call Darren, the man from town who prunes our trees? He knows about these things. He keeps bees himself. Perhaps he'll even come up and help you. His number's in my phone.'

Ted found the number and scribbled it down, then went back outside and sat on the wooden bench under the maple tree on the lawn, his favourite place for thinking. Would he really need to ask for help from a professional beekeeper or could he simply move the bees himself? How hard could it be? The bees seemed to respond well to him.

But then the pain of the bee sting he'd experienced as a child reared up in his memory. Maybe it was best to call Darren first.

He dialled the number and heard Darren come on the line.

'Hello, Darren, Ted here,' he said. Then, without waiting for a response: 'Listen, I was wondering. Hypothetically, if someone found a swarm of bees near their house, should they catch them?'

'Definitely not,' Darren replied. 'Well, not on their own. They'd need quite a bit of help. There's a real art to bee handling. They can be aggressive if they're disturbed.' He paused then asked, 'Are we talking about *you* finding a hive? Is that what you're saying?'

'No, not me,' Ted replied, chuckling. 'I was only asking because I heard of swarms of bees being found at this time of year and I was wondering what to do if I ever came across one.'

'Well, you'd need a beekeeping suit and a few bits and pieces, but it can be done. For someone like me, it's pretty easy. Get a bin or a box and sit it under the swarm, give them a gentle nudge with a stick and they'll fall into the bin like water. Once they're all in there, slap the lid on. But it's dangerous if you don't know what you're doing. So why don't you call me if you find one?'

'Okay, will do. Thanks, Darren.'

But Ted had already made up his mind. Despite all he'd just been told, he would move the bees himself. There was a large cardboard box in the garage and an empty beehive in the corner of Martha's yard. He would steer the bees into the box and transport them to a new home.

He packed the box into the car, along with an old hiking stick, and headed back to the gum tree. As he cautiously stepped from the car, he was certain he heard the sound of the swarm shift down in pitch again. They were happy he had returned.

He took the box out of the car and placed it next to the swarm, then picked up the stick. But he couldn't bring himself to prod the bees with it. That seemed just plain unfriendly. So he stood quietly and contemplated his next move.

Meanwhile, the sound of the swarm changed again, and there seemed to be more movement within the seething mass. Then some of the bees began to drop down into the box and settle on the bottom. It was magic. He felt they could sense his intentions, without him saying a word.

Standing perfectly still, he whispered, 'Stay calm, I'm taking you to your new home.' Sure enough, the ball of living bees began to pour down into the box like water, until they were all inside.

Ted had no intention of locking them in with a lid. Instead he just lifted the box, assuring them as he did so that if they weren't happy where they were going, they would be free to leave. Then he carefully placed the box in the back of his car, gently shut the hatchback, got into the front seat and turned on the engine. As he drove, the buzz of the bees became louder.

'Don't worry, you guys,' he reassured them. 'This is how we humans get around. We don't fly like you do.'

Soon, a few bees emerged from the box, then more and more. But they weren't trying to escape, and Ted felt confident they wouldn't harm him. They settled all over the car's interior: on the roof, on the steering wheel, on his arms and even on his face. By the time he arrived at Martha's, the car had turned into a moving hive, and he felt he was part of the family.

Covered from head to toe in bees, Ted staggered to the corner of the yard and stood in front of the empty hive. One by one, the bees flew off him and circled the hive. Ted kept perfectly still until all his passengers had left. Then he went to the car, removed the box containing the remaining bees and placed it next to the hive. Before long, it seemed all the bees were in flight around the hive, as if waiting for a signal to land. Ted could feel the air moving as they brushed past him, but he still felt completely calm.

That was when he saw her. Bigger than all the others, she was sitting quietly on the sleeve of his shirt, as if she was assessing the situation. The queen. Seconds later, she gently lifted off from his arm and landed gracefully by the entrance to the hive. She was magnificent.

As she moved into the hive, the bees began flying in ever-widening circles, as if getting to know their surroundings. Then, over the next fifteen minutes, they all entered the hive. Ted could hear a deep contented hum emanating from inside.

Once he was sure all the bees had settled, he walked back to his car. A spring had returned to his step, and he whistled quietly. He stopped to marvel at the sunlight streaming through the trees and the music of the birds, then turned to check on his new friends once more.

When Ted got home later that day after feeding the chickens, he moved calmly into the sitting room, sat down in front of the television and turned on the Discovery Channel.

Janet watched him, clearly puzzled but pleasantly surprised. Neither of them was sure what exactly had occurred that day, but they both knew that life had just got better.

# Strip the Willow

Jane likes to get involved in the culture of any country we visit, and she was keen to do the same during one of our recent stays in Scotland.

In Morocco, we stayed in a riad and paid a visit to the souk to shop for carpets before going out to the desert to ride camels by day and camp by night. Surrounded by shifting sand hills, we sat drinking mint tea and feasting on a méchoui, a whole sheep roasted on a spit, while watching exotic belly dancers shimmy in the moonlight. We have gone into the jungle-clad hills of northern Thailand and spent the night in caves, cross-legged and meditating, with a hundred chanting Buddhist monks all dressed in orange robes and the scent of burning incense filling the air, before building fires early next morning and making food in pots so large we had to stir the dishes with paddles made to propel a boat. In the south of France we have travelled to the coast near Cassis and dived from the rocks into the dark blue Mediterranean waters to find fresh sea urchins, then eaten them straight away while sipping local rosé made from grapes that were grown no more than a hundred yards from where we sat.

So it only made sense that in Scotland we should try to take in a bit of my cultural heritage. After some research, Jane jumped at the chance to organise a visit to a Scottish knees-up. 'I have booked us all into a Scottish cultural show,' she announced. 'It should be fantastic. I think I'll wear my kilt in case we have to dance for our supper.'

She was excited at the prospect of sharing the event with me and her parents, John and Phorn (a Thai name short for Gusumphorn), who happened to be touring Scotland with us at the time, and delighted that she seemed to have found a bargain. 'It's amazing, Jimmy. The show only cost ten pounds for the whole group of us.'

This immediately got me wondering. 'So, I guess for that price we won't be watching this cultural show in an old castle.'

Jane suddenly looked a bit crestfallen. 'It is very inexpensive, isn't it?' she replied. 'Maybe I should have looked a little closer at what the show offered. I hadn't even thought about it like that. It said it was in a hotel. I assumed it would be in the ballroom of a grand old place with turrets and high walls, but given the price that does seem a bit unlikely.'

Despite these concerns, we decided to take a chance and go along and see what they had to offer.

As we pulled into the car park, it became apparent that this was definitely not the kind of hotel Jane had hoped for. It was old, but far from grand. The building reminded me of the Kariwara, a hotel my father used to drink in back in Elizabeth West in South Australia. The Kariwara was not known for its cultural shows, unless you think that bar-room brawls with people crashing through the doors and out onto the streets are cultural.

We stood outside the car, wondering whether to go in.

'Are you here for our show then?' A loud voice snapped us out of our thoughts. A somewhat dishevelled man was tucking a shirt with puffy sleeves into his kilt as he stepped from the car parked next to us. 'Come on, just follow me and I'll show you where to go,' he said as he wiped food from his crumpled clothes and beard. Even from ten feet away, we could smell the whisky coming from his breath.

'Aye, all right,' I mumbled. 'Let's go then.'

It seemed we were trapped and there was no way out of it without insulting the lowly Highlander, so we followed at a safe distance behind him, whispering to one another.

'If it's really bad, we'll just leave,' promised Jane.

There wasn't much chance of it being good, when I thought about it.

We walked into the hall and I immediately felt my shoes stick to the floor. I'd performed in cleaner places when we were first starting out in the music business and would play anywhere for money.

Our tickets were checked by a young girl who turned out to be related to the Highlander.

'Aye, aw right then. Off ye go tae yer seats. Ma da will be with ye soon. Just sit where ye like. Best if ye get close tae that dance floor in case ye want tae get involved in the show.'

We immediately went as far from the dance floor as we could. Jane's father took one look at us and knew what we were thinking. Ever the career diplomat, John had no intention of starting an international row while we were in Scotland. 'Listen, you two. We are here now and we can't get up and walk out. It would be rude. They are very proud, strong people, the Scots, and they will take offence. So just sit there and have your drink and take it all in.'

Jane and I looked at each other and did what we'd been told.

The room slowly filled with old folks, many of them in wheelchairs. It looked like they were bussing pensioners in from nearby care homes for the show. There was no way they could get up and run out, even if they wanted to.

My legs felt restless, but soon it was too late to leave. Besides, John continued to make it clear he was staying put.

'Righty oh. Let's get this show on the road,' shouted the raggedy Highlander as he jumped out of his chair and onto the dance floor. A woman who appeared to be his wife turned on a cassette player that sat on the table next to them – and he was off dancing and shouting his way around the room. It appeared that the whole cultural show would be performed by this couple.

'Yahoo! Aw right then, let's make some noise now,' the showman hollered.

The wife turned up the cassette player until it nearly exploded. The sound of poorly amplified bagpipes filled the air as the host jumped from table to table, lifting his kilt up and scaring the customers. It seemed it was true what they said about kilts: go combat or go home.

Jane, in total shock, buried her head on my shoulder and whispered, 'I need to get out of here. Now!'

I leaned over to John, who was tapping his foot to the music and pretending to be entertained. 'John, I think we should go.'

But he was too polite to walk out. 'Listen, you two, just sit there and be nice.'

Phorn sat watching the show, the blood slowly draining from her face. The hairy, unkempt Scotsman swished past her, flicking up his kilt.

The old ladies from the home were visibly thrilled and shrieked every time he repeated this move. Apparently this was much better than the bingo outing they'd gone on the day before.

Next the showman circled the room, singing a song about midges – tiny biting insects that torment residents and visitors alike during the Scottish summer. He became ever more manic and was scanning the audience, looking for another victim to shock. The thought of getting drawn into the act terrified me.

I turned to Jane. 'Right, we are out of here.'

Jane and her mum conferred and it was settled, we were doing a runner. Now we needed a plan.

John was still digging his overly polite, diplomatic heels in and refusing to move, but Jane had already decided that he would have to be sacrificed. If he really wanted to stay, he would be on his own.

By now the showman was dragging able-bodied people up to join in a dance called Strip the Willow, which involves at least four couples lined up with the men facing the women. The top couple move down the line, the woman swinging round each man and then her partner. Then they make their way back up, with the man swinging round the ladies and his partner, and finally they come back down the line, the lady swinging with the men and the man swinging with the ladies in between swinging with each other. Cue next couple. Got it?

Jane jumped up, grabbed her mum's hand and led her to the dance floor. As she and her mother danced, they moved closer and closer to the exit sign.

I realised I was being sacrificed along with her father, so I jumped up and followed them across the room. When we got to the exit, I banged on the rail and sent the door flying wide open. Then, before you could say, 'Put that thing away before I smash you,' we were out the door and running across the car park, laughing hysterically. We got into the car, sat down and breathed deeply. PTCSD or Post Traumatic Cultural Stress Disorder as it is better known, was slowly settling in on all of us.

Before long, Jane's father followed us out and sat down quietly in the back seat of the car. He wasn't happy. 'Well, I hope you're satisfied,' he finally said. 'You embarrassed the hell out of me – and you made me miss the rest of the show. It was just getting good when you mob ruined it.'

We drove back to our immaculate country hotel in total silence. It was so good to get back to our clean rooms. Jane jumped straight in the shower and tried her best to scrub off the residue of our 'cultural experience'. The show wasn't mentioned again until we got back to Australia. By then the great distance between the performers and ourselves made it all seem much funnier.

Strip the Willow has been retired from our dance cards. We won't be needing it again. Jane no longer harbours the romantic idea she once had of buying a little cottage in Scotland by the sea. If I'm still that way inclined, she tells me, then I should get a *really* wee place, because she won't be staying there with me.

# Songs Frae Hame

| | |
|---|---|
| '9/8 March & Jigs: Bathgate Highland Games / The Hills of Kazakhstan / The Fiddler's Rally' | BOGHALL & BATHGATE CALEDONIA PIPE BAND |
| 'Strip the Willow' (medley) | THE SCOTTISH FIDDLE ORCHESTRA |
| '3/4 Marches: MacGregor of Rora / Lewis a Turrell's / Killworth Hills' | SCOTTISHPOWER PIPE BAND |
| 'Donald Where's Your Troosers?' | ANDY STEWART |
| 'By the Water's Edge' (slow air) | SHOTTS & DYKEHEAD CALEDONIA PIPE BAND |
| 'Loch Lomond' | THE PIPES & DRUMS OF LEANISCH |
| 'Comin' Through the Rye / Dram Behind the Curtain' | EDDI READER |
| 'Skye Boat Song' | THE PIPES & DRUMS OF LEANISCH |
| '93rd at Modder River' | THE PORRIDGE MEN |
| 'The Highland Laddie' | THE TANNAHILL WEAVERS |
| 'Dashing White Sergeant' | GORDON PATTULLO'S CEILIDH BAND |
| 'Scottish Soldier' | STEVE MCDONALD |
| 'Scotland the Brave' | MASSED PIPES AND DRUMS, ROYAL EDINBURGH MILITARY TATTOO |
| 'I Love a Lassie' | SIR HARRY LAUDER |
| 'Amazing Grace' | COMBINED MASSED MILITARY BANDS AND MASSED PIPES AND DRUMS, ROYAL EDINBURGH MILITARY TATTOO |
| 'Wild Mountain Thyme' | ELLA ROBERTS |
| 'Auld Lang Syne' | THE ROYAL SCOTS DRAGOON GUARDS |
| 'Flower of Scotland' | THE BAND OF THE SCOTS GUARDS |

# The Sorcerer

My father was a boxer, but he was also an enchanter, a Scottish sorcerer of sorts. When I think about him these days, I remember him dressed in a suit and tie like a real showman.

He might have even worn a top hat and a cape too, though I could be wrong about that. I always wondered how he could influence the way so many people behaved with just a wave of his hand or a look in his eye. The effect was most pronounced on us kids. A gentle shift of his glasses, from low on his nose – which was surprisingly straight for a prize-fighting wizard – to a position high on the bridge of that very same perfect nose, brought his dark eyes into focus, and suddenly we were under his control.

It was like a superpower. He could immediately see through us and into our very souls. He knew exactly what we were up to, what we were planning and what we were hiding. And we would stop what we were doing and succumb to his will.

That same movement seemed to turn on a lie-detector, too. When his eyes were clear, he could see everything and we would do whatever he asked us to do, whether it was to go to bed or get ready for school, or even tell him what Mum had been saying about him when he wasn't there. It was like he had waved a magic wand and cast a spell on us.

I realised, as a child, that he had the same profound effect on older people too. He could charm them into doing whatever he wanted. At least until they got to know him better. On one occasion I watched as he turned an aggressive debt-collecting woman, who had banged on our front door demanding we pay one of our many unpaid bills, into an admirer, with just a simple shift of his eyebrows and a tilt of his head.

For a long time I believed he could even work miracles. I half-expected to see him walk on water, and I certainly observed on many occasions that he had a knack of turning water into wine, or even whisky if required.

Dad created illusions. He had a way of making a bad situation seem like something special. On one of the many times when our electricity was turned off and we were left sitting in darkness, shivering, he thought about the situation for a few moments then came up with a plan.

'Right, kids,' he announced, 'listen to me. We're all going on a camping trip!'

'But Dad, where are we going? We'll no find anywhere to camp at this time of night.'

'We're going tae camp right here on the floor of the lounge room.'

Then he began throwing blankets onto the floor and building a makeshift tent out of the sheets that covered the holes in our second-hand couch. Once we had settled into our campsite he huddled us together so he could make an announcement. 'Okay, kids, I want you all to stay right here and guard the camp while I go out to hunt for provisions and get hold of a few wee things to help us ride out the storm.'

'But it's not raining, Dad.'

'Hey, don't question me. I know what's best for you lot.'

'Aye, okay, Dad.'

Off he went, quietly into the night. Somehow he got waylaid en route to the general store by the bad weather that no one else had seen coming and had to take refuge in the local tavern with a bunch of his mates. We didn't see him again for a few days. But we knew his intentions were good, and camping can be a treacherous pastime.

Sadly, there came a time when his magic didn't seem to work anymore. The first to notice the change was our mum. I knew that for a long time he'd had some special mind-control over Mum, but it gradually wore off. She was too tough.

She told him, 'I'm not falling for any of your fucking tricks anymore.'

At that moment, I remember thinking to myself for the first time, 'It was all tricks? Oh no!' Had his magic really been all smoke and mirrors? I was shattered.

But that was when he pulled off one of his biggest tricks ever: he made Mum disappear. We all kept waiting for her to come back, but she didn't for a few years. Dad looked like he was quite happy with himself for a while, but then

My dad, Jim Swan, eventually lost his cloak of invisibility and was forced to stick around. I think he was happy to lay the wand to rest.

his smile disappeared – along with everything else we had: our hopes, our dreams, our happiness.

Eventually, Dad was just a shell of the magician he'd once been. His cloak, his wand and his top hat were replaced by a booze-soaked, unpressed shirt and ill-fitting pants with pockets full of pawn-shop tickets, tokens of the only things of value that had ever occupied our house. During this period it seemed that the only time I saw those eyes that had once worked such magic was through the bottom of a whisky glass. Bleary and red, they had lost their mojo.

A few years later though, in an act of defiance, and just to prove he still had powers, Dad pulled off another miracle. One afternoon he made Mum reappear in our lives. At least we thought he'd done it.

We were so happy that she was back and hadn't been sawn in half that we never saw what was coming next. Dad had one final illusion to pull off. In a puff of Rothmans Plain cigarette smoke, he disappeared from our family home once and for all. Maybe this was the greatest Harry Houdini impersonation ever. In a single brilliant movement, while suspended high above the frozen river that was his empty life, he shook his way out of the chains that bound him inside the trunk of his unhappy marriage, picked the lock that shackled him to his children, and was gone. We would have brought the curtains down then and there, but Mum had pulled them off the windows one night a few years earlier during a fight with Dad, when she wanted to burn the house down.

I stopped believing in magic for a long time after that, until my own children came along. Now I know that anything is possible.

# Shirley Knott

I remember my father telling me that the only soldiers Hitler feared were the Gurkhas – those brave fighters from Nepal who joined the British army – and the ones who wore skirts.

By the latter, he clearly meant Scottish soldiers, and, like my dad, I had long thought that if I ever had to go into battle I would want Scots on my side and no one else. But as I grew older and my view of life broadened, I began to question that assumption. Because increasingly it seemed to me that the men who wore skirts and were the bravest I had ever met were not bagpipe-playing, battle-hardened, afraid-of-no-one Scottish soldiers but a bunch of really tough drag queens who worked in the bars along Oxford Street in the eastern suburbs of Sydney around the turn of the millennium.

Prominent among them was Steven, though his Sydney friends called him Shirl and Shirley Knott was his official drag name. Shirl had moved to Sydney from way up northwest, in Narrabri, in cotton country, when she was young, running away from a world where she didn't belong. Running to the bright lights of the big city, like a moth to a flame.

I got to know Shirl through going to the clubs with friends and was lucky enough to be considered a friend.

In those days, roaming gangs of so-called straight men tried to infiltrate the gay bars of Sydney in search of trouble, or maybe a taste of something wild. And boy did they find it – those clubs were as wild as they came, and their drug-crazed clientele didn't take well to outsiders invading their turf, so strangers entered at their peril.

I watched Shirl regularly as she marched fearlessly into battle with complete strangers on the dance floors of Sydney's best hot spots, dressed only in a frock and high heels. It didn't matter how dangerous the night became, she would face it down, standing tall and defiant in the spotlights that seemed to follow her as she made her way through the darkened clubs, ready to fight.

Shirl had stared death in the eye even before she got to Oxford Street. Every time she walked the streets alone on her way out on a Saturday night, she took her life in her hands. Sydney had a reputation for being tolerant, but we all heard the rumours or saw the news stories on television about young men going missing and being found smashed against the rocks that lay below the treacherous cliffs close to Sydney's most famous beaches.

Carloads of drunk young men from the suburbs, out to prove how strong and butch they were, often cruised the grimy Darlinghurst streets in search of victims to torment, and anyone was a target, especially if they looked at all stylish or overtly happy. So a young man strutting down the street in a bright yellow off-the-shoulder dress, matching shoes and handbag was the ultimate prize. What better way to show your friends in the car how brave you were? But many a foolish young goon met his match when he encountered Shirl. Standing over six feet tall from the point of her heels to the top of her highly lacquered and extremely flammable hair, she was a sight to behold. She could peel the paint from a passing car with her blood-curdling voice and she was afraid of no one.

'Darl, you can't be serious. I've literally eaten better men than you for breakfast. Now piss off before I sink my stiletto into your scrotum. Go on, get. That's right, you heard me, boy, fuck off.'

And she meant it too. Country town prejudices had forced her to fight all her life. She had become hardened beyond belief by the time she learned to sew her own sequins on her first dress. She'd been beaten by bigger men, and always lived to dance another night. So a spotty teenager, wet behind the ears, full of beer and bravado, was no match for her. She could take him down with one blow of her tongue.

Those were the easy battles she fought on a regular basis, but there were darker demons to be faced by the end of each night. Alone and filled with pills and poisons that most people hadn't even heard of, she would cry as she peeled off her war paint and became Steven again.

Steven was shy and wounded. The boy who was afraid of everything and had to be at work in an office within the hour would stand naked in front of a mirror crying as the sun climbed into the cold, grey morning sky. How long could Shirl keep fighting their fight? One of them had to go sooner or later, and maybe both of them were running out of time.

As all his friends used to say, Steven was too tough to be a man and far too frail to be a woman, so they straddled the blurred line between the two. Shirley could out-drink, out-dance, out-party and out-fight most people, but it still wasn't enough to fill the emptiness she felt inside when it was only Steven in the room. So she had to be more. More outrageous. More outspoken. Wilder. But, in turn, this approach was killing Steven and they both knew it. Every step she took forward moved him one step closer to the edge. Soon he was standing on a precipice, staring down into the abyss.

Eventually, Shirl decided she had to swallow Steven up once and for all. He could never be seen again. He was the chink in her armour and she was the anchor tied to his leg. She had to find a way to support the two of them. That would be better. Then it would be her life, and Steven would be gone forever.

She found a job working the door in one of the clubs of an old friend. She towered over all who entered, welcoming some but warning most. 'In you go, darl, but don't start any trouble or you'll have to answer to me, the door bitch, okay? I'll give you a right old flogging if you do. Of course, it'll cost you double, but it'll be worth it.'

Night after night, she stood in the door with her eyes pinned wide open, like Bambi in the headlights of an oncoming car. Thanks to the make-up she wore, no one ever noticed the wear and tear that was beginning to show on her face. The longer she worked, the more her drug intake increased. Uppers, downers, horse tranquillisers – it didn't matter to her as long as they numbed the pain. After a few months she started turning up late for work on the odd night. Then those nights became more frequent, until the day she stopped showing up at all.

We tried dragging her out for dinner to cheer her up, but she was too damaged to be reached. Concerned friends would go to her home and find her still dressed in the frock she'd worn the night before, mascara running down her face, stubble pushing through the pancake make-up, unable to stand up, never mind leave the house. She stopped answering the phone or noticing the constant knocking on her door, until eventually her friends stopped visiting and she was left alone. A few people caught a glimpse of someone they thought was her – a pale, skeletal figure quickly pulling the curtains closed – as they walked past her house. I heard Steven even got another day job for a short time, but it didn't last.

Finally the day came when they were both gone. The word on the street was that Shirl had gone back to Narrabri, but I couldn't believe that – she hated the place.

But those in the know said she'd had enough and had gone back to die.

Time passed and Steven was completely forgotten; his light just faded away. But Shirley still burned bright in stories they told on the Sydney streets, stories of a supernova, a dazzling star that blinded Saturday night sightseers on the Sydney sidewalks, of a hurricane that swept down Oxford Street on a stifling hot summer's night, trailing a cool, soothing breeze that blew through the doorways. And young men who came to the big smoke to disappear from somewhere else and find a new life in the city heard about her in the bathrooms of Stonewall and other clubs as they powdered their noses, flicked back their beautifully teased locks, straightened their tits and smeared glitter onto their lips, readying themselves for another big night on the dance floor.

# Learning to Love the Old Girl

In the late 1960s, when I was young, my mum got married for the second time, to a man from Port Adelaide, and we moved to a house near the Port River.

My new stepfather was a good man and after the troubles Mum had had with my real father I was happy for her to find some peace. My stepfather, who was Port Adelaide born and bred, wanted to be close to his ageing parents so he could look after them. I didn't mind because the idea of living near a river appealed to me for many different reasons.

So far, I'd spent most of my childhood in my bedroom and I wasn't used to an outdoor life, except for when I was wearing soccer boots and running around with a ball at my feet. But I'd always dreamed of fishing and surviving on whatever I caught. It didn't concern me that I knew nothing about the sport. Someday I'd learn.

The only problem I had was with the Port Adelaide River, or the Port River as it was known locally. It looked like the dirtiest river in Australia.

I asked my new grandad, Bill, about it.

'Don't worry, son, she's a working river,' he reassured me. 'They're all a bit dirty. That's part of her charm. You'll love her when you get to know her.'

Then he told me that the Port River was actually a tidal estuary and not a river at all. I said that surely in that case it should have been washed clean by the tides, but that didn't seem to be happening. He replied that I asked too many questions.

Soon after, at school, I learned that most of the kids in the district would at some time over the summer swim in the river. I was shocked. I imagined that after one decent dive into the water, you might never surface again, and, if you did, you would surely have contracted dysentery.

I was keen to find out all I could about the river, and one day when I was at home my grandfather, between sips of tea, began to tell me more about the 'old girl'. From then on he continued to speak of the river as 'her', like someone he had a relationship with, and from the way he spoke so fondly about her I could tell he knew every secret she kept. I'd never seen him look happier.

He told me how he'd spent most of his younger days somewhere along her banks, trying to catch fish. Sadly, he could no longer make it to his front door, never mind the riverbanks. He loved Port Adelaide and he described the Port River as the lifeblood of the community, the beating heart of the district. 'You know, son, this place started out as a mosquito-infested wetland, and, like everything in this world, it was changed, and not necessarily for the better. Over the years, the local government tried to make the waterway into a port. We locals all laughed. At one time we called the town Port Misery because, in spite of all the work they did, the river was still nothing more than a swamp. But they dredged and dug and dragged the bottom for years until the waters ran deep enough to carry the huge cargo ships that move up and down her today.'

He paused for a few moments, lost in memories.

'After that she was worked really hard,' he went on. He described how the ships full of cargo travelled the length of the river, their noisy diesel engines spluttered and choked, coughing out thick black smoke, and their props churned the water to a muddy mess. 'The landscape changed too, and within a few years we didn't recognise the joint. Factories popped up along the banks where we used to fish. Chimney stacks blocked the sun and billowed smoke across our town. Day and night, the factories pumped wastewater and God knows what else into the poor old girl. It all took a terrible toll on her, but somehow she survived.'

'But did people still fish there?' I asked.

He explained how, while waiting for the bad weather that would blow up in the gulf to pass, fishing boats often wound their way between the ships and barges into the heart of the town. While the fishing crews were in port, they could get the fish they'd caught off the boat and into the market. And they could easily walk to one of the many pubs that lined the back streets for a well-earned drink – there was no shortage of pubs in town. 'But most of the fish they sold at market weren't caught at our end of the river,' Grandpa Bill continued. 'They came from out in the deep waters of the gulf. They used to say anything that was hooked up our way was no good for eating. Said those fish would glow in the dark and should be quickly tossed back into the old girl to die. But what did they know? We locals never worried about that kind of thing. We were thrilled to catch any sort of fish at all, and we weren't throwing them back for love or bloody money. Our fish would be taken home and scaled and eaten before you could say stomach pump.'

He turned and looked at me. I could see he was enjoying telling me stories about the old girl, so I smiled and nodded, urging him on.

'Then they built a bloomin' power station on the riverbank, close to the mouth, and spilled even more crap into the river. Pipes poured hot water and chemicals straight into the water. The poor old girl became a dumping ground. In those days there were always strange characters hanging around the wharfs, doing all sorts of dodgy deals. Dead dogs and cats used to float by me as I sat on the banks. I even heard stories of bodies being dumped in the river. Nothing surprised me, and it didn't bother me. I still loved the old girl.

'And the weird thing was, the fish seemed to love her too. I fished there for a little while, before I got scared off by some nasty blokes up to no good, and I used to catch tommy roughs by the dozen. They reckoned there were some really big fish to be caught after the power station was built. Mulloway, snapper and salmon as big as a wharfie's arm were pulled out of the Port, and the blokes who caught them regularly bragged about them. I tell ya, they were dangerous times to be in those pubs. The wharfies just wanted to wind down after a hard night's work, and didn't take well to the fishermen bragging about their catches. I kept well away from those places, but I heard stories of ripper fights that even the police were too scared to get in the middle of.'

I could see he was getting tired and the excitement of reliving the past was wearing him out. I needed to go and explore the river for myself. After Grandpa Bill's stories, I didn't want to go near the port, and anyway my rod couldn't have coped with the really big fish he said were found there. I would stay local, within walking distance of Grandpa's house, and start with the less appealing, much slower-moving Old Port Road end of the river. I still wanted to fulfil my dream of surviving on the fish I might catch, but was a bit worried about eating them after all I'd heard. Grandpa reassured me that he'd never known anyone to get sick from the old girl's fish. That was good enough for me.

The first day I went out, I discovered what I was sure was a secret path that led from the side of the Old Port Road down through spindly salt bushes, over the rocks that stop the high tides from flooding the bridge, and along the bank of the river. It took me towards the Causeway Bridge, a two-lane crossing that connects the end of the Old Port Road with the smaller streets of the proud working-class suburb of Ethelton and, further west, to the long sandy beaches north of Adelaide. At that time, the Port River stopped running here and slowly crawled back into the stagnant swamp it once was. There had been no need to dredge this far down because no big boats would ever come here. (Later, ten million tonnes of mud were excavated to create today's West Lakes.)

I realised this was one of those secret fishing spots I'd heard some of my school friends whisper about, the locations of which were passed on quietly from fathers to sons. No one was going to divulge family secrets to a newcomer like me – I'd just stumbled across it by accident – but I felt in my bones that this was the best place for me to fish.

As I followed the path, the silence was broken by the high-pitched scream of a spinning reel, followed by the splash of a baited hook as it plummeted into the murky river. I turned and saw a salty, leather-faced old man casting and retrieving his baited line. As he lifted his rod up and down, working the bait, his cropped T-shirt revealed his bare arms, just skin and bone covered in washed-out blurry blue tattoos, bleached by a lifetime in the sun. Below the lopsided cap that sat on top of his head, his eyes were unblinking blood-red slits that looked like they'd been carved into his gaunt, weather-beaten face. They stared, cold and hard, never once leaving the point where his line met the water. A hand-rolled cigarette balanced on the corner of his blistered lips, glowing bright as he took a deep breath, smoke billowing out each time he exhaled. He never looked at me once.

I could tell that he was expecting something special to take the bait any minute, so I decided to wait and watch, even if it meant being late for the last day of school before the summer holidays. It wasn't long before a loud splash broke the peace of the morning and a silvery bream sparkled in the sun as it leaped from the cloudy river into the air. I held my breath and watched as he fought his prey, his rod buckling under the strain of the life-or-death struggle, until he landed the fish on the riverbank. It was only after he'd safely placed it in a bucket of water that he turned his gaze my way.

'You like to fish, do ya, son?' A toothless smile spread across his wrinkled face. He looked pretty happy with himself as he waited for my response.

'Er, yes, but I'm a beginner, not like you.' Then I was lost for words. In my head, though, I made a mental note to come back to this place and try to catch a fish just as he'd done.

I stood and watched as he packed up his gear and got ready to leave. 'Is that you done for the day?' I asked, finally finding something to say.

'Can't eat more than one fish a day. So, yeah, I'm done, I guess. See ya again.' He turned and walked away.

The very next day, I went back there to fish from the Causeway Bridge, hoping for as good a catch as the old man's. After what seemed like an hour of preparation, I threw out my very first cast. To my horror, I heard the line snap and the top half of my rod detached itself from the rest of my fishing rod, sailed through the air and disappeared into the swamp. I was left holding the handle and not much else.

As I set off down to the river to look for my gear, I spotted another path that was completely invisible from the road. Curiosity got the better of me and I decided to take a look and see where it went. It took me down to the river's edge, roughly where my gear had disappeared. Then I noticed that the path appeared to continue across the adjacent clearing and along the bank, becoming narrower and more treacherous-looking.

I had to follow it. I found the top of my rod down by the rocks, then carried on walking. Soon the path was lined by jagged rocks covered in razor-sharp barnacles. One false step and I would be cut to ribbons. Eventually I arrived at a spot just below the old railway bridge. I was soon knee-deep in foul-smelling thick mud that sucked the shoes right off my feet every time I took a step. Something told me that I was getting close to where the best fish in the whole of Port Adelaide could be caught, that the railway bridge might allow me to reach it, and that this secret spot could be mine and mine alone.

The bridge had clearly seen better days. It was rusty, decrepit and hard to scale. Surely no one else would be mad enough to climb up on it? I decided to stand under it for a while and watch as the trains crossed. Every time one neared, the screaming of metal on metal, as the driver hit the brakes before the train sped into the bend that led onto the bridge, was deafening. Next, the bridge started to shake, as if an earthquake was tearing it apart. I watched in amazement, wondering how the whole structure didn't collapse into the river. Then there was silence.

Between trains, I studied the river, looking for signs of life. Fish regularly broke the surface, seemingly to feed, then dived deep whenever another train approached, which seemed to be about every quarter of an hour.

The blood was pumping through my veins. This was the most alive I'd felt in my short life. I decided then and there that this was where I would spend my summer holidays. Alone on the railway bridge, waiting to meet the biggest fish in the river.

Day after day, I returned and climbed the treacherous girders that supported the bridge to a spot where I could safely sit, directly above the place I felt was the prime target, where the river ran at its deepest. Waiting for bites that never came, I sat there alone, staring off across the water, deep in thought. I thought about fishing and I thought about my life.

From time to time my imagination took me on wondrous escapades. There was no one else around for miles, and I pictured myself living completely alone there, doing whatever I liked and eating only what I caught. I would build a shelter below the bridge at the side of the river, just something strong enough to keep out the rain, and I'd sleep there until I caught the biggest fish ever seen in the district.

Every now and then I would be rattled back to reality by a train thundering down the tracks and across the bridge as I held on for dear life. But then it wasn't long before the train was gone and I was lost in thought again.

Other people would appear on the river, but they never seemed to stay long. Some clearly came just to see how far they could go up the river – and were quickly disappointed. Early one evening, I saw two men pull their ute up at the wharf not a hundred yards from the bridge and begin emptying two forty-four-gallon drums of fluids into the already murky water. Whatever was in the drums left a green film across the surface. Local kids came to swim in the river, oblivious to what was being poured into it, but thankfully no one got too close to the bridge. One morning I spied on a bunch of shady-looking men in a dinghy as they stopped and fiddled with something they held low beneath the lip of the boat. They seemed to be lighting things with matches. Then they tossed objects that looked like fireworks into the river, a loud dull thud sounded and water spouted high into the air. I realised they were using dynamite to fish. Stunned bream and flathead floated to the surface and the men, laughing loudly, scooped them into a net and onto the boat. There would be no fish left in the river if they kept this up. I never saw them again that summer, but no doubt they had a few favourite haunts.

Each morning I followed the path through the mud to my secret spot and each evening I plodded back along the path empty handed. I had taken to making sandwiches and taking a Thermos of tea so I never went hungry. Some days I stayed until after the sun went down to see if the fishing was any better, but getting back to the causeway was perilous enough in broad daylight, never mind in the dark. At night I lay awake thinking about what I would try next. Was I casting wrong? Was it the bait I was using? I asked other fishermen I met, but they gave me no clues. I read books on fishing, but it didn't help. I still caught next to nothing, and the fish I did catch were too small to take home without running the risk of being laughed at.

Days rolled by, soon the summer was nearly gone and I began to feel a chill in the air. I knew my expeditions were coming to an end and I would very soon have to give up my quest and start to think about school. A few days before the new term started, when I headed down to the causeway and reached the river, there was another person fishing there. It was the old man I'd met just before the school holidays. As I walked by, he looked up at me.

'Have you been catching anything from that railway bridge?' he asked.

'How did you know I've been fishing there?' I shot back.

'I've been fishing the Port River since I could walk, and I know everything that happens here, boy. Besides I used to fish from that bridge when I was young like you. I only stopped because it's too hard for me to climb it now.'

I could see tears well up in his eyes as he spoke. 'That's where you'll get something special, young fella, if you haven't already.'

'I haven't caught a thing from the bridge, even though I'm sure there are fish under there,' I replied.

'What are you using for bait?'

'I buy a different bait every week and none of them make any—'

'Hold it right there, son.' He wheezed as he lit another rollie.

'What do I call you?' I asked politely as he lit his cigarette.

'Will. Nice and short and easy to remember. It's really Wilfred, but only my dear old mum, God bless her soul, called me that. What'll I call you?'

'Jim. My mates all call me Jim. But it's really James. Only my mum calls me that, and only when I'm in trouble.'

'All right, James it is. What you have to understand, James, is that most people will use whatever bait they are given. The bait shops will tell you a load of old rubbish. All they want to do is sell their cheap bait that'll work in most places. But fishing is a very specific business. Each place has a bait and rig that works best. If you want to catch fish here, you've got to know what the fish want. What are they after, swimming around in this part of the river? What exactly brings them this far?'

'That makes sense, but how would I find out?'

'Well, if you let me finish, I'll tell ya. You have to keep it to yourself though, or everybody will be dragging fish out of the river day and night till they're all gone. My fishing days are nearly over, so it makes no difference to me, but to an eager young angler like yourself, learning about the right bait could mean the beginning of some real fishing in the Port. Do you follow me?'

I nodded and moved a little closer.

'Anyway, it'll be good to pass it on. I used to catch bucket-loads of fish in my day. But back then we needed them or else we didn't eat. My dad would scale them and Mum would fry them up. She knew how to cook a tommy rough better than anyone I ever met.' He seemed to be lost in thought for a moment, then continued, 'So I'll do you a deal. If I pass on my secrets to you, you won't take too many fish from the river. Only what you can eat.'

He stopped and looked me in the eye. 'Do we have a deal?'

'Yes, sir.'

'Who?'

'Er, I mean Will.'

'Deal.' He shook my hand. 'You found the path through to the bridge, obviously. But have you had a look at what's lying around out there?'

'There's nothing but mud.'

'That's right. So whatever those fish are after must be living in the mud, right? Every time that tide comes in, that mud is covered by the water. That's what those fish are waiting for.'

'But what are they eating?' I asked.

'Tomorrow morning, early, when the tide is out, if you meet me here, I'll show you. Bring a bucket and a shovel with you. And, oh, you're going to get pretty dirty.'

He said his goodbyes and walked slowly away. That night I could hardly sleep. Would I finally have a chance to catch a big fish from the bridge?

I was standing by the river before the sun had even come up. As the first rays of light peeped above the horizon, the old man walked slowly towards me. He held a strange-looking tyre-pump kind of thing in his hand.

'Morning, James. Looks like a great day for fishing. I've never seen a bad day for fishing, mind you.'

'What you got there, Will?' I asked, pointing to the metal pump.

'This, young fella, is going to make fishing easy for you. It's a bait pump. Follow me.'

We made our way down to the path around the rocks and along the bank until we reached the mud flats.

'This'll do us right here. Now, look carefully and tell me what you see,' he said, pointing to the mud.

'Well. There's a lot of mud, I guess.'

'Look again, son, and look a bit closer.'

It was early and my eyes were still adjusting to the light. But then I noticed something peculiar. 'There are holes, like little tunnels in the mud.'

'That's right, boy. And they're made by blood worms,' he whispered.

'Should I be worried?' I mumbled.

'No, they can't hurt you, if that's what you're asking. Anyway, what you've got to do is take this end of the pump and shove it into one of these holes.'

I pushed the pump into the mud. It slid in effortlessly until the mud came almost to the top of it.

'Right, pull the handle up as far as it will go and then take the pump out of the mud.'

I followed his instructions carefully.

'Now put the end into the bucket and pump the mud out.'

As I did so, I saw that as well as mud there were long red worms in the bucket.

'There you go. Good as gold. You've got yourself some of the best bait you can find, right there. Just be careful when you pick them up 'cause they have pincers near their mouths and they might bite you. It won't kill you, but it feels a bit weird.'

We continued to gather worms in the mud flats until I had enough to last the day.

'Right, son, the rest is up to you. If you can't catch fish with that bait, you never will. All you've got to do is rig up a hook below a running sinker, feed the worm onto it, and Bob's your uncle.'

'Aren't you going to come up with me?' I asked.

'No, boy. I've shown you all I can. It's up to you now.'

He wiped the mud from his hands, turned and walked back along the track towards the causeway.

I could hardly wait. I grabbed my gear and the bucket and clambered up to my fishing spot.

As I cast my line that had just been rigged, weighted and baited perfectly, everything seemed different. I was no longer uncomfortable on that rickety old bridge. I was in the right place and I knew what I was doing, for the first time in my life.

My bait splashed in the water and sank below the surface. Even before it hit the bottom, I felt an almighty tug. My rod bent in half as I began reeling in the line, before my quarry dived deep and I had to hang on for all I was worth. The battle went on for what seemed like hours, but was probably only ten minutes or so. Then, finally, just as my strength was fading, I watched in amazement as a huge silver bream broke the surface of the water and shimmered in the morning light.

# An' Scotland Drew Her Pipe an' Blew

When we were children in Adelaide, my father always tried to instil in us a strong feeling of pride in our Scottish heritage.

He maybe thought it could be a tool to help us survive in the tough new world we had moved to, but I suspected it came from an overwhelming sense of loss my parents felt on being forced to leave their families and homeland behind forever. They couldn't have really wanted to emigrate halfway around the world to a country they knew very little about, and I believed the move was more about my mother's need to escape her own personal problems. She wanted to leave behind the shame of her upbringing and start a new life where no one knew her history. And she hoped she and Dad might even find a good life for themselves, and for their children. But the reality was they never escaped anything.

I sometimes wondered if Dad championed all things Scottish to make my mother feel guilty for dragging him away from where he belonged, the only place where he'd felt any sense of self-worth. In Glasgow he was a champion. In Glasgow he was a hardman. In Glasgow he was feared. In Glasgow he could stand tall. Anywhere else, he couldn't. In Australia, he was just Jim Swan, another lost immigrant looking for a new life.

Anyway, for whatever reason he did it, my father always wanted to share his love of all things Scottish with us. Shortbread was the best biscuit ever made. The St Andrew's Cross and the Lion Rampant were the only flags worth fighting for. The Scottish soldier was the toughest, most feared warrior in the world. And, of course, whisky was mother's milk, the drink that could keep you warm on the coldest nights, inspire you to sing the praises of the old country to anyone who'd listen, and help you stand up and fight no matter the size of the enemy you faced.

So you won't be surprised to hear that one of the highlights of his year was when the Royal Edinburgh Military Tattoo, held in the city's magnificent castle, was broadcast on late-night television in Adelaide. Military bands from all over the world travel to the tattoo to perform with bands from the British armed forces in an amazing international celebration of the unconquerable Scottish spirit.

For some reason the television station didn't transmit the event until long after it had actually happened, in August, perhaps because they didn't have the technology to broadcast live in those days, and they usually held it over until the week between Christmas and New Year. Given that it's such a festive event, that must have seemed the best time.

I always loved the tattoo for several reasons. One was that it meant we got to stay up late and watch television, which was always good. Another was it brought to a halt any fights between Mum and Dad. A third was that it seemed to make Dad inordinately happy, though that might have been just due to the fact that for once he got to sit down in front of the television without being lectured by my mum and drink a whole bottle of whisky by himself. It also gave them both a chance to imagine being back in the place that was their real home.

From childhood onwards it was a dream of mine to see the tattoo in Edinburgh and I finally got to do that a few years back, with the love of my life, Jane, by my side. We booked the 'Gatehouse' package, which included an early dinner within the walls of the great castle. The room was dark, moody and memorable, and the meal was even harder to forget, for different reasons, which included paying seven hundred pounds each to be herded around like Highland sheep with a pack of drunken Americans, and dishes that had probably been devised back in the days when the Empire was still relevant. It did mean, however, that we got to walk through the castle's massive oak doors and across the drawbridge to the Esplanade – the same route the mass pipe bands would follow to enter the tattoo. That was very special.

The tattoo is held at the height of summer in Scotland and August is usually the warmest month, when there's a decent chance the weather will be kind. It wasn't. I remember being offered a blanket as we sat down, a sign of things to come. As the first of the bands entered the arena, the temperature dropped faster than the sun sank from the sky, and soon the rain began to fall. But I must

On our way to the tattoo. Jane has always been a sucker for a man in a kilt.

say it only added to the beauty of the spectacle. A thousand pipers coming through the mist was breathtaking. I sat mesmerised as they marched triumphantly around the parade ground, playing songs that called to me from my childhood.

The highlight of the evening was most definitely the lone piper who closed the show. A single player, standing alone and defiant on the wall of the magnificent old fortress, staring down the wind and rain and the changing times, while playing a melody that was both haunting and heartbreaking. I never for a moment dreamed that Jane would be so moved by the show that she would later play bagpipes on stage in my band. What a girl.

That night my heart was full, and as the piper played and the St Andrew's Cross waved in the howling wind high above the turrets of the castle, I thought back to those days when we sat at my father's feet and dreamed of what life might have in store for us.

I love it when Jane gets up on stage with me and plays the bagpipes.
It's like my own private tattoo. *(Debra Fitzsimons)*

# Lifesavers

My brother John and I lived together a lot during my younger years. As I have said in the past, I looked up to John. In my eyes, he could do no wrong.

John was wild and funny but also very caring and protective of me. He got me out of trouble on many an occasion. But just to be clear here, he had a fair bit to do with most of the trouble that I got into as well. Not all of it – I was very good at starting trouble myself – but a lot of it. I looked up to him, and in most situations I felt I was safe when he was around.

I have documented the fact that I hung around in gangs when I was a teenager, quite often getting into trouble and fights. I know now that I would never have made it through those years if John had not been in the picture. Most of the people I knew as a young hoodlum would give me a wide berth rather than take on John. He was dangerous – vicious but fair was how I used to describe him. So, I think I really owe him my life.

Besides starting trouble, I only learned how to sing because of the help and guidance John gave me. He played the best music to me in my formative years. He was the first person to introduce me to blues music: Muddy Waters, Little Walter, Paul Butterfield and Bo Diddley were just a few of the artists he played in his room back in Heytesbury Road. When his friends were not around, ten-year-old me would even be allowed into his room to listen to this wondrous music with him. As I grew older and his musical world evolved, so did mine. I remember one day when he couldn't wait to play me a new artist he had found.

That's John playing the drums in this photo of his first band, taken at the
Elizabeth shopping strip.

'You have to hear this, Jim. This is where music is going. This guy is the future,' he said as he played *Are you Experienced* to me for the first time. The sound of Jimi Hendrix's guitar changed the way I looked at music forever.

Later John got me into southern US bands like Edgar Winter's White Trash, whose album *Roadwork* was a huge influence on my style of singing. John also played a young Stevie Wonder to me: *Uptight* was a regular on his early playlist, as were albums by The Jackson Five and the Temptations. I remember him sitting me down a few years later and dropping the needle onto the *Talking Book* LP, a record by a more mature Stevie Wonder – he must have been all of twenty-two years old when it first came out. It changed the way we all thought about music.

As we grew older, John and I often lived in the same houses in Adelaide. He felt it would be easier to keep an eye on me that way. The places we rented were never luxurious: we had a limited budget, and what money we had we needed to keep for party supplies. We stayed in some real dives, but we were always well supplied. Cold Chisel were a young, struggling band at this point, so I wasn't making much cash, but John was playing in covers bands that were getting a lot of work, and he put up most of the money for our accommodation.

Our houses were always party central. No matter where we were, come closing time, John and I were never ready to stop and go to bed. We thought sleep was overrated and that the party always had to keep rolling on – normally at our place. Sometimes it lasted for days on end. Fuelled by copious amounts of booze and cheap drugs, John and I would outlast most people in town, even those who thought they could really party. There were a few exceptions – I remember Bon Scott drank me to the ground a few times – but there weren't many who could do that. Hardened drinkers would arrive at our house after closing time, all talk and bluster, only to be carried out by their friends, vomiting, as the sun was coming up. Meanwhile, we'd be already on the lookout for the next party, then we'd kick on until the sun went down.

On most such nights one of us would have a show to do. I would go and sing with John, or he would come and sing with me, and then we'd party. If time permitted, we would sleep for a day or so, then start all over again. This went on for years. It was exhausting, but, hey, we were only young once. Getting old was overrated too, we thought. Live fast, die young and have a good-looking corpse – that was our motto.

John and I both ended up in Sydney around the same time in the mid-seventies, and we very quickly fell into the same routine when we got there. By this time the stakes were much higher. Both of us, despite our wild behaviour, had promising careers. The right people were starting to take notice of us. John was in a band called Feather, an offshoot of the famous Sydney band Blackfeather. The famous music publishing and recording company Albert Productions was very interested in them. And there was a buzz around Cold Chisel, due to the incendiary live shows we were putting on almost every night of the week – though friends also worried about how long we could possibly keep it up.

After shows we would usually end up at the Bondi Lifesaver, our favourite Sydney watering hole. The core clientele consisted of record company executives, aspiring models and drug dealers. So, it should come as no surprise that it was the place to find rock musicians too. This club launched, and also saw the dying days of, a lot of musical careers.

It could be a dangerous place. If you crossed the wrong person or spoke to the wrong girl, you could end up feeling the wrath of the overzealous bouncers, who were more than happy to send you off in an ambulance. We hung out in one or two of the corners, where we could get up to no good in the shadows. Most of the punters were too scared to come anywhere near us.

It became such a regular haunt for us that John and I decided to move into a very small, run-down apartment

Can you tell how much I looked up to my big brother? With John in 1977.
*(Lorrie Graham/Sydney Morning Herald)*

practically adjoining the place. From the front door of our flat, you could look over the fruit and veg shop below us and almost through the front door of the Lifesaver. We would watch who was going in, and when someone we knew or needed to see, like a drug dealer, turned up, we would walk down the stairs and straight through the front door and the festivities would commence.

We became friends with the managers, the bouncers, the barmen, the kitchen staff and even the cleaners, so we knew the people who opened the bar and those who were last to leave. After the place closed, we would sit with the bar staff and drink till sunrise. It seemed they had all taken a shine to us. Which meant we could always get something to drink or a line of coke if we needed it. They were lifesavers too. Sometimes I wondered if the club used most of its profits to keep the music industry supplied with booze, but I found out later it was really only John and myself and maybe one or two others who got this special treatment.

Food was never a priority, but on the rare occasions when we needed to eat we could quite easily jump from the top of our stairs into the front courtyard of the fruit and veg shop, where they stored the produce, and grab a pumpkin or two to see us through the week. John had picked up a great recipe for pumpkin soup while he'd been a cook in the army, and we survived on that for most of the time we lived there. Whenever we made money, we would go down to see the shop owner and apologise for stealing his goods. He would laugh and send us on our way: he knew what we were up to and didn't seem to mind.

It was a crazy lifestyle. Many of our friends ended up drinking themselves to death or overdosing alone in seedy hotel rooms, or, even worse, committing suicide. But John kept me under his wing and steered me through the madness and around the pitfalls of the music industry. Although a similar lifestyle would later take its toll on me, looking back on my youth I can see that John was my saviour for most of that time, until I was old enough and smart enough to make my own decisions. We both made it out by the skin of our teeth and somehow, astonishingly, we are both still here.

# Swanee's Soundtrack

| | |
|---|---|
| *Are You Experienced* (whole album) | Jimi Hendrix |
| 'You Really Got Me' | The Kinks |
| 'White Room' | Cream |
| 'Bo Diddley' | Bo Diddley |
| 'Killing Floor' | Howlin' Wolf |
| 'I'm a King Bee' | Muddy Waters |
| 'Hey Joe' | Jimi Hendrix |
| 'Sunshine of Your Love' | Cream |
| 'Mannish Boy' | Muddy Waters |
| 'Leland Mississippi Blues' | Johnny Winter |
| 'I'm a Boy' | The Who |
| 'Tin Soldier' | The Small Faces |
| 'Hurdy Gurdy Man' | Donovan |
| 'I'm a Man' | Chicago |
| 'Spinning Wheel' | Blood Sweat & Tears |
| 'Albert's Shuffle' | Al Kooper and Mike Bloomfield |
| 'Substitute' | The Who |

# What's New, Pussycat?

It was back in the late eighties, at a show in a club on the Gold Coast, the Las Vegas of ... No, wait, I take that back. It was never the Las Vegas of anywhere really.

Back in the eighties the Gold Coast was a cultural desert. A shithole. There were always lots of people moving through the place, either on holidays, searching for the perfect lifestyle by the sea, or running from the cops. It was a weird crowd. You could get a suntan, learn to meditate and have your wallet stolen all on the same weekend. The place had everything.

Anyway, on this particular night, just before I went on stage I got the word from my production manager, Sneaky Pete – an ideal name for someone working on the Gold Coast – that Tom Jones was coming to the show. Now, I'd long been a big fan of Tom. He had, and still has, a huge Welsh tenor voice and an even bigger persona, and he always came across as a funny guy, someone who worked hard and didn't take himself too seriously. So I got excited, and my mind went into overdrive thinking of things I would say to him, like, 'Hey, Tom, I guess girls throw themselves at you all the time. Like … it's not unusual?' Those kinds of things.

The whole night while I was singing I was picturing my band, a very tough rock 'n' roll band, playing 'Green, Green Grass of Home', and trying to work out exactly how we would do it and which bits I would sing. The thought of standing on a stage next to Tom and just doing my usual screaming didn't seem right to me. I knew I'd have to dig deep and find another voice that better suited the occasion. At first I searched for that Scottish

Tom Jones is not just a great singer, he has so much more than that – style, charisma, whatever you want to call it. *(Getty Images)*

coal-miner tenor buried somewhere deep inside me, but when I found him I remembered why he was locked away, and moved on.

I couldn't miss the chance to bring Tom Jones on stage with me. But what song could I get him up to do? Tom was essentially an old soul singer. He even sounded a lot like another of my favourite singers of all time, Levi Stubbs from the Four Tops. In fact whenever I listened to 'Walk Away Renée', it reminded me of Tom. So I immediately started thinking of soul songs to do. It was a late show on this particular night, and Tom was arriving about midnight … Bingo! I would sing 'Midnight Hour' with Tom Jones.

I ran to the side of stage and instructed Sneaky. 'When Tom gets here, ask him if he wants to get up and sing.'

'He might be tired, Jimmy,' Sneaky replied. 'I think he's already done a show and had a late dinner.'

'I don't care. He's fucking Tom Jones. Ask him.'

As it got close to midnight, Tom still hadn't showed, and I began to get a little nervous. If he didn't make it, I would be hugely disappointed. But I also knew what it was like: people have the best intentions, but after a big dinner and a few drinks you often just feel like getting an early night …

Not Tom. I looked up after the next song, and there he was: Tom Jones, standing at the side of my stage, next to Sneaky Pete. Now, Sneaky is not a big guy, and Tom was towering over him and resting his elbow on Sneak's shoulder. I had to laugh.

Tom seemed happy too, very happy. He stood there smiling and waving to people in the front row. At least half my audience – the female half, essentially – were already either passing out or pulling their underwear off, ready to throw at him. Would this stop him getting up on stage? It didn't seem like it, as he was still smiling and nodding and giving me the thumbs-up, busting a few moves while I sang. Even members of my crew started fainting.

As the end of the set loomed near, I invited Tom onto the stage, and the crowd went crazy.

For some reason, Sneaky accompanied Tom to the middle of the stage. Then, as the audience continued roaring, Sneak pulled me aside and whispered, 'He's out of his mind.'

'What?'

'Why, why, why did you insist on getting him up here?' Sneak asked.

'What? I can't hear you.'

'He should be seeing the green, green grass of his hotel room.'

'What are you saying, Sneaky? Spit it out.'

'Tom is *really* drunk!'

'No, that's Tom Jones, he never gets really drunk. But I am, so get off my stage and let me sing.'

Sneaky shook his head and walked away.

I'm here to tell you, if Tom was drunk, I never noticed, because he sang like a demon. Like a man possessed. I'd been screaming for two hours and sounded a bit like a man repossessed, but fortunately no one noticed as Tom tore the house down. (He's still doing this today, by the way – I recently saw a sprightly eighty-three-year-old Sir Tom Jones put on a storming show in the New South Wales Southern Highlands, fuelled by nothing more than healthy food and mineral water.)

Backstage afterwards, Tom chatted away and was charming and funny. A real gentleman. We drank my rider dry and it must have been two hours after the concert finished when he finally said his goodbyes. 'Well, Jimmy boy. That was a fabulous night, but as I have two shows tomorrow I'd better be off before you find us more to drink.'

'It was great to sing with you, Tom,' I said. 'But tell me, I've often asked myself how you keep that big voice of yours going. What's your secret?' We singers all have secrets, and I wondered if I could get him to share some pearls of wisdom with me.

'Well, you see, Jimmy, it's very easy. I just open my mouth and it seems to come out.'

'You don't gargle or anything?'

'Not really. Maybe with a little cognac, but that's about it. Though I do carry three humidifiers on the road with me at all times. That seems to help.'

He staggered away, bouncing off half of the walls backstage.

Sneaky turned to me and said, 'If that fellow can sing and have girls throw themselves at him even in the state he's in, I reckon there's hope for all of us blokes.'

'No. He's fucking Tom Jones. It's like a superpower he has, Sneaky. He really should have a cape.'

For the rest of the tour I had three humidifiers placed in every room I stayed in. It didn't help a bit. I think that was a little joke Tom tells every young vocalist he meets. Night after night, all over the world, there are probably singers sweating buckets as they lie in their beds. Thanks to Tom.

*A Visit from Steve* Cold Chisel gathering to rehearse for their fiftieth-anniversary tour. Left to right: Phil Small, Charley Drayton, me, Ian Moss and Don Walker. *(Daniel Boud)*

*A Visit from Steve*
'He's right there …
next to me.' With
Steve Prestwich at
Megaphon Studios,
Sydney, 1997.
*(Robert Hambling)*

*Trouble in the Rearview Mirror* Jackie acting as chauffeur. We were living a rustic life in the Southern Highlands of New South Wales, but the family still liked to travel in style. This was our second Mercedes, c.1988.

*Across the Tracks* Jane sampling haggis at our dinner in Glasgow with our Scottish relatives, including, to my left, my cousins Jackie and Jim, and my newly discovered uncle from Canada, Archie.

The Texas Tornado Jam
The line-up for the show near Austin on 11 July 1981, one of my favourite US gigs ever and the start of many musical friendships. Good to see we were at the top of the list.

*The Texas Tornado Jam* Backstage before the show with my dear friend and legendary roadie Gerry Georgettis. Gerry did sound for Cold Chisel for many years, as well as for other great Australian bands. *(Rod Willis)*

*An' Scotland Drew Her Pipe an' Blew* The Royal Edinburgh Military Tattoo was definitely one of the highlights of our recent visits to Scotland. *(Shutterstock)*

*What's New, Pussycat?* Catching up with the great Tom Jones at the Byron Bay Bluesfest, Easter 2024. *(Mahalia Barnes)*

*Old Haunts* The Gleneagles hotel in Perthshire has always been one of our favourite places to stay in Scotland. *(Shutterstock)*

*Old Haunts (right)* We first went to Gleneagles when the kids were wee. A home away from home? If only!

*Old Haunts* Our search for a perfect Scottish residence led to a magnificent manor in North Berwick, east of Edinburgh, where most of our clan gathered for Christmas in 2017. That's my son-in-law Jimmy in the bearskin hat.

*A Unifying Sound* The Stray Cats on stage. Left to right: Brian Setzer, Slim Jim Phantom and Lee Rocker. The Cats are one of my favourite modern rockabilly bands and I was proud to have them as my support act on a tour of Australia in 1990. *(Alamy)*

*A Unifying Sound* In the studio with The Living End in 2004. Left to right: Scott Owen, Andy Strachan, Chris Cheney and me. A shared interest in rockabilly culminated with Chris and me forming The Barnestormers with Slim Jim Phantom from the Stray Cats and piano legend Jools Holland. *(Getty Images)*

*A Walk on the Dark Side* The Royal Mile in Edinburgh's Old Town, the starting point for our ghostly tour. *(Shutterstock)*

*A Walk on the Dark Side* The entrance to the graveyard at Greyfriars Kirk in Edinburgh, target of grave robbers in the early 1800s and supposedly one of the most haunted places in Scotland. *(Shutterstock)*

*Our Precious Time* Steve always drove us hard and kept us on track. Thinking about him, as I do often these days, reminds me to make the most of the time I have left. *(Getty Images)*

*Highways and Byways* All roads lead back to home and family. At Eliza Jane and Jimmy's wedding in the Southern Highlands in 2024. I grab any opportunity I can to wear my kilt. Left to right: David Campbell, Mahalia, Elly May, me, EJ, Jane, Jimmy and Jackie.

# The Crystal Radio

So tired. I can hardly move my body. I'm drifting in and out of dreams. I hear a distant voice, faint amid white noise. It seems to be calling to me.

I try to respond but can't find the words. I can't even remember where I am. Then the voice fades, and a sharp creaking sound brings me back to the present.

*Sproing.* The springs of the bunk bed above me come into view. They bulge and stretch and strain like they are about to snap under the load of my big, substantially overweight brother, Gary. My heart sinks as I realise he's still wide awake and looking for trouble.

'Are you having a little baby nap down there, you stupid little rat, you?'

Then those big gorilla paws he calls hands, the same ones that hit me most days, wrap around the frame of the bed above me. He's on the move. By the light of the moon that softly glows through the window, I can make out a sneering, puffy face and big, bulging eyes scanning the lower bunk, checking for movement. Seeking a target.

'Hey, you, Francis, short stuff. I know you're awake. You'd better answer me and you'd better do it quickly or I'm coming down.'

I roll over to face the wall, but I know that if I don't answer he will jump down and punch my arm until it goes numb. He plays this game with me every night until he gets bored. I'm not allowed to sleep until he sleeps. I think he is scared of the dark but doesn't want me to know it.

*Sproing.* How can such small springs support his weight? Something has to give. I can tell he is about to get up and pay me a visit, so I answer quickly, 'Y-y-yes, I'm awake. Wh-wh-what do you w-w-want?'

It's funny, but I only seem to stutter when I'm extremely nervous or when my brother picks on me. He knows it, and the sound of my trembling voice only makes him more determined to mock me. The bed above me creaks and groans again. Those springs are surely about to snap. What a way to die. I can see the headlines now: BOY CRUSHED IN BIZARRE BUNK-BED ACCIDENT.

'N-n-n-nothing,' he mocks. 'I just want to k-k-keep you awake, you s-s-stupid little d-d-dork.'

He laughs to himself again as he swings his big paw towards my head. I can feel the breeze as it swooshes past my nose. One of these days he'll break my face and the bed.

'Anyway, what are you whispering for, dumb-ass? Mum's working nightshift at the factory and Dad's asleep in front of the TV. He can't hear us. You could be shrieking and begging for help, and he wouldn't hear you. So answer me when I talk to you or I'll give you something to really scream about.'

I look at the clock on the bedside table. It's 9.30. We've only been in bed for forty-five minutes, though it seems like hours. But I know he'll get bored with me soon enough and drift off to sleep. Then I can get on with the night I've planned.

Gary likes to hit everyone. Especially me. He and his bully friends pick on me and my friends all day at school. They call us dweebs. They tease me about my name: 'F-F-Francis, that's a girl's name. Hi, F-F-Francis, nice dress you're wearing.'

He always tries to make me cry. But I never do. When I'm at home, I just run to Dad.

Dad knows how to cheer me up. Sometimes he takes me into his office and turns on his CB radio. He says it's his way of staying in touch with the world. Rolling the dial, he finds people from all over the place to talk to. He says there are ham operators like him everywhere. I've had a few lessons from him, but he reckons I have a long way to go.

'You might like to start with a crystal set, son,' he told me. 'They're simple and easy to use. They even have an earpiece so no one else can hear what you're doing.'

Dad knows when Gary has been picking on me, and he tries to console me. 'You know, son, your big brother is a bit dumb. A brick short of a load. He gets that from your mum's side of the family, not mine, by the way. Oh, and don't tell her I told you that. You know what I mean? It's our secret. We don't want to start trouble, do we? You're smart like me, son. So just try to keep away from him. And, no matter what, don't let him get to you.' Then he usually winks at me, laughs and tells me to get out of his sight.

So here I am, waiting for Gary to fall asleep. You see, I have something to do, something he doesn't know about. No one does. I've saved up all my money. Well, when I say 'all my money', it's not actually *my* money; it's money I found on the floor, where Dad throws his trousers in the laundry for Mum to wash. Not much each time, just a few coins here and there. But it all adds up. After work, Dad is always so tired he doesn't notice the small change in his pockets. So it's not like I'm stealing. I just happen to find the coins lying there.

Yesterday I counted my money and I finally had enough to buy the one thing I've really wanted. A crystal radio set. Just like the one Dad told me to get. I'd seen it advertised on a poster on the wall of the local electrical shop a few months earlier as I was walking home from school. I go into that shop all the time. I like gadgets, you see. Anything with wires and valves that light up will get my undivided attention. In bold red letters the poster said: *The newest device on the market. This tiny radio is the latest thing in 1960s technology. Handmade in Tokyo, Japan. The way of the future. No wires. No batteries needed. Tune in to the world — and maybe even worlds beyond!*

I had to have one. It was so small I could hide it away under my mattress and listen to the outside world at night when I was alone. The words on the poster set my mind wandering. I wondered what they meant by 'even worlds beyond'.

I told the shopkeeper to put one aside for me, but that it had to be our secret. I said it was a present for my brother's birthday, even though I would never buy him anything like it. He wouldn't even know what it was, let alone how to use it.

This afternoon, on my way home from school, I went to the shop and handed over my money. Now I can't wait to get started. Tonight, when Gary goes to sleep, I will tune in for the first time.

Dad used to tell me, 'There's a great big world out there, son, and one day you'll see it.' I want to see it all. A world where no one chases you home after school, no gangs try to beat you up, and no big brother tries to pull your underwear up so high it hurts. Where I can listen to radio broadcasts all night long.

*Sproing.* The springs scream out again as Gary rolls over, and then they are silent. I think they have either been beaten into submission or he is finally asleep. I lie still and quiet, pretending to be asleep too. He could be trying to fool me.

When I can hear long, slow breaths, I reach under my mattress and pull out the radio. The whole set fits into a small paper bag. The unit itself is not that big, just a little box with a dial on one side for tuning into the stations.

There are two wires coming out of the radio. One leads to the earpiece, the other to an alligator clip. All I have to do is attach the alligator clip quietly to the springs of Gary's bed above me and stick the earpiece in my ear, and I will be able to tune in to the world.

I open the bag, trying not to make any noise, but the sound of crumpling paper cuts through the silence like thunder.

*Sproing.* Gary groans and whispers something muffled about Miss Ellery, the pretty young redheaded sports teacher from our school, turns over and is soon sound asleep again. I pull the radio from the bag in one movement, then pause, listening. Nothing, he's gone this time. My heart is racing. I take a deep breath and clip the radio to the spring above me. I place the earpiece in my ear. There is no sound. I roll the dial slowly with my thumb and listen. Still nothing.

Suddenly my earpiece comes to life, just for a second. I hear a scratchy, hissing sound, but still no voices, before all is silent again. I unplug the alligator clip and wonder what to do next. I move it to a spring closer to the open bedroom window, which unfortunately is directly underneath Gary's head. Straightaway the tiny speaker crackles and whistles in my ear. I move the dial, searching for a clear signal, and that's when I hear a voice for the first time.

'This is the BBC World Service. Now it's time for the World News.' It's the same voice I heard when Dad listened to his wireless in his office.

I keep searching the airwaves. There's another sound, something different. But I've moved the dial too fast and it's gone as quickly as it appeared. I slowly turn the knob back. There it is. A man's voice, but not like the BBC announcer. This voice is different, muffled and frightened. It grabs my attention instantly.

'Hello, hello. Can you hear me. I need help. I need he—'

Again, it's gone. What was that? Was it a distress call? It sounded like one. My eyes dart around the room. Did Gary hear it? No, he's still out cold. But I'm wide awake now.

I quickly roll the dial again, trying to tune back in. There it is again, and the signal is clearer this time. The voice, echoey and booming, sounds like it's coming from inside a cave. 'Hello, is anyone out there? Can you hear me? Please, I need help. I'm not going to make it. Oh, damn it, somebody answer me, please!'

Then the voice is gone. I turn the dial back and forth over the same spot, but there's no more sound. All I can find is the BBC newsreader.

Who on earth was that? Where are they? Why were they asking for help? Where were they trying to escape from? And ... haven't I heard that voice before somewhere?

I turn the dial again and again, but eventually tiredness overwhelms me and I give up. I unclip the radio, roll up the wires and place the set back in the bag. Then I carefully hide the whole thing under my mattress once more and drift off.

I'm jolted out of a deep, deep sleep by the sound of my mother's voice and her hand shaking my feet as she walks past my bed. She pulls the curtains apart and the sun beats mercilessly on my face.

'Up you get. It's a beautiful day out there and it won't wait for you.'

I fall out of bed and drag myself to the kitchen table. Mum has prepared breakfast for us. She must be exhausted after working all night, but every morning when she comes home she gets us up and makes breakfast. Even with her bloodshot eyes, she looks beautiful and happy.

'You seem tired this morning, son. Are you all right?' she asks, not really wanting an answer. We're always tired.

I nod, mumble something indecipherable and tuck into my scrambled eggs.

School that day drags on and on. The sun hitting my back as it shines through the classroom window makes me sleepy. I can feel myself nodding off, and have to fight it.

'So, at that time, people thought that the sun and the other planets revolved around the Earth. We were the centre of the universe ...' Our teacher, Miss Irish, is reading to her attentive class, but unfortunately my universe is closing down. I shut my eyes, only for a second, but it's long enough for her to notice.

'Excuse me, are you asleep in my class?' Miss Irish asks.

I jolt awake, and as I look around I see that all the eyes in the room are on me.

'It appears that Francis thinks this lesson is too boring. So we will stop now and continue with it tomorrow – when Francis will explain the whole chapter to you in detail. Isn't that right, Francis?'

I can see the disappointment in her eyes. After all, I'm her best student and have never fallen asleep in her class before. No one has. No one would dare.

'Y-y-yes, M-M-Miss. I-I will.'

The bell rings, signalling the end of the day. I run to my locker, grab the books I'll need to prepare my talk, and leave the building. My mind is on one thing and one thing only: the voice on my crystal radio. I want to race straight home on my bike, get all my chores done and get to bed early.

But as I leave the school grounds, the sun is suddenly blocked out by the hulking silhouette of my brother's enormous friend Maca. I know at that moment that Gary and his dim-witted mates are waiting in ambush.

I try to turn my bike in the other direction and head to the back gate, but I'm too late. In an instant, they're all around me.

'Hey, F–F–Francis. Have you g–g–got a–a–any m–money f–for us?' Gary taunts me.

'Why don't you just leave me alone? I just want to get home and do my homework,' I say. 'Okay?'

'Oh. Hear that lads, goody two-shoes here wants to get home and do his homework. Well, what's the hurry? Surely you have something for your dear big brother?'

*Thwack.* His enormous mitt crashes into the back of my head.

'I know you've been saving up your pocket money, F–F–Francis. I saw you counting it the other day. So, come on, hand it over.'

'Er, I–I–I s–s–spent it already.'

'Oh, he spent it already. Is that fair, guys? I bet it was sweets. You've always got a stash somewhere. Come on, hand them over.' He turns to his moron mates, who by this time are drooling at the thought of tormenting me even longer. 'You guys like sweets, don't you?'

'N–No,' I inform him, 'I b–bought a c–c–crystal r–radio.'

'A crystal what? Is that some sort of jewellery, or something for your girlfriend?'

'N–No, and I–I–I don't have a girlfriend.'

'Don't answer me back, small fry.'

He raises his hand to slap me a second time, but I've readied myself and I manage to duck the blundering blow. I bounce back up before he realises he's missed me, jump onto my bike, swerve past the slow-witted gang all desperately trying to grab me, then tear off down the footpath at breakneck speed.

I ride home, sit at the table and get out my books. Mum is at the kitchen counter, making sandwiches to eat on her break at work.

'You're home early today. You got no friends to play with, son?'

'No, Mum. I have to do a presentation to the class tomorrow, so I'm making sure it'll be great.'

'What a clever lad. Getting asked to do something special for the class. That teacher must love you, especially with your high grades and all. You must be her best student.'

'Er, yes, Mum. That's right, I'm her favourite student.' Mum works so hard I don't want to tell her I'm in trouble.

'Well, I'm off to work. I'll see you in the morning for breakfast, my clever boy.'

'Right, Mum. See you then.'

I feel so bad lying, even if it's just a white lie, but I don't want her to worry about me. Besides, I need to get my homework done – and avoid my brother – so I can be free later, when the coast is clear, to get on my radio.

Come bedtime, I have to wait for Gary to drop off before I can start, but it's not long until he's sawing logs.

I quietly remove the radio from the bag and attach the clip to the bed springs. I put the earphone in and turn the dial. I think I hear the voice again, but it's so crackly and distant that I still can't make out what it's saying.

I lie in bed and wonder what to do. Then it comes to me. Gary was right about one thing. Dad would by now be asleep in front of the TV, for sure. He works so hard all day at the factory that after two 'cheeky whiskies' as he calls them, it doesn't matter what's on the telly, he's soon out cold, snoring in his chair. He won't budge until midnight, which gives me about two hours to sneak into his office and turn on his radio. Maybe I can find the voice of the man in trouble on his radio.

I roll out of bed, trying not to make a sound, and crawl across the floor, keeping my head as low as I can. Gary doesn't move an inch. The next bit is harder: getting out the door without the light in the hallway shining into the bedroom and waking him. In one swift movement I open the door slightly, slip through the gap and close the door softly behind me. I head down the hallway, but unfortunately my second step finds our house's one creaky floorboard. The noise is so loud I almost jump out of my skin. I stand perfectly still. Surely someone heard that? I wait, hardly breathing, then carefully move on. Finally, I make it to the office, step in, close the door behind me and turn on the small lamp.

I've used the radio many times before, but never without Dad's help. I sit for a moment and try to remember what to do. Dad always says that everything has to be done right or it won't work. I find the power switch and flick it on. The meters light up. Slipping on Dad's headphones that he bought from the second-hand shop, I start turning dials. At first I can hear only white noise. I sit for another half hour, twisting and turning every knob and then, out of the blue, I hear a crackle and a call. I slow my movements, and listen like I've never listened before.

'Hello. Hello, is anyone there?'

It's the voice from the cave again. I reach for Dad's microphone, hold it close to my lips, press the button on the bottom of the stand, and say softly, 'Hello. Can you hear me? Hello.'

There's no sound for thirty seconds or more. But then I hear the voice again.

'Yes, I'm here. Can you hear me? I need help.'

Once again, the voice sounds strangely familiar.

'I'm trying to lift my hand,' it continues. 'I can't seem to move at all. Please, help me.'

This time I'm certain I know the voice but I can't place it. Is it a friend of Dad's? It sounds like his brother, but he never uses a radio.

'Are you still there? Tell me where you are.'

'I'm still here … I can't … breathe … It's agony … Please, do something … I really need help, please.'

The voice is softer now. He sounds like he's rapidly getting weaker. I'm overwhelmed by the terrible feeling that if I don't help him soon he won't survive. I reach for the microphone again and press the button—

The room is suddenly filled with blinding white light. So bright it burns my eyes. I close them quickly and hold them shut as tight as I can. I'm overcome by a sharp, unbearable pain in my chest. A cacophony of sounds fills the room. Bells are ringing, machines are buzzing. I can hear voices but can't understand what they're saying.

I slowly work up the courage to open my eyes again. I'm no longer in the office but lying on a bed. Above, I can vaguely make out the faces of people huddling over me. The faces are masked, but their eyes are clear and caring.

'He's coming round,' I hear one of them say.

A gentle hand touches my face. 'Francis, can you hear me? You're going to be all right. We'll give you something for the pain.'

A man moves close to me, then the world turns black again. Next time I wake I see a nurse moving around the room, quietly and purposefully. Then she notices that I'm looking at her and her eyes light up, and I know she is smiling below her mask.

'Where am I?' My voice is weak and scratchy.

'You're in intensive care. You've just had major surgery, but everything went well. It's nice to see you back with us, as you've been out for a while. But you're in good hands here and you're going to be all right. So, you just need to relax. Shall I turn the radio on for you?'

# The Darkest Hours

My brothers and sisters and
I have never really recovered
from our childhood. It's a time
best not remembered, if that's
even possible.

We were always there for each other until the day we weren't. One minute all we had was each other: we were totally interdependent, ready to die for one another. We covered our ears to block out the shouting, huddled together in the darkest corner of the room so we didn't get hurt. Then suddenly, in what seemed like the blink of an eye, we grew up, and now we speak to each other only when we really have to. It isn't because we don't want to talk anymore; it's just too painful when we do.

Any conversation could drag one or all of us back to those times that we want so much to forget. You see, our childhood, as painful as it was and as hard as we have tried to work through it, still lives inside us. No matter how firmly we keep our eyes on the future, the past is always right there, waiting below the surface of our extremely thin and damaged skins. A tiny scratch and it bleeds out, and the suffering starts all over. A word, a thought, a picture, a song – the simplest of triggers can send us reeling and spiralling down to despicable depths. It's a dark, disturbing feeling that twists and distorts everything that is important to us. It can blind us so much that we can no longer even see love. See each other.

Listen to me, talking for the family when I should be speaking only for myself. I have no idea what really goes on in my siblings' minds, but when I look into their eyes I can sense the same pain that I feel.

A rare shot of all the siblings together, showing the hope we could muster when we needed to. Left to right at back: Dorothy, John, me and Linda; Alan and Lisa are at the front.

Our parents never meant to hurt us, it just happened. They were caught up in their own pain so much that they lost sight of us and we just got in the way of their escape. That's what they were doing, escaping. My dad tried to do it by drinking himself into oblivion. It didn't work for him and eventually he buckled under the pressure, dragged my mother down with him and they both fell apart. We were simply written off as collateral damage and left to bleed, literally and metaphorically.

And what were we left with? A sense that we would never be good enough. Good enough for what you might ask. Good enough to be loved. Good enough to be trusted. Good enough to be wanted. Good enough to walk with our heads held high. And with that lack of self-esteem came a feeling that nothing good that we had would ever last. Sooner or later, it would disappear. So why wait around for that to happen? Better to cut the cord and walk away on our own terms than continue to suffer that endless anxiety.

This was how I lived for most of my life. Hyper-vigilant, hypersensitive, hyperactive. Just hyper really. Enduring every moment like I was waiting, head on the block, for the guillotine's bloody blade to fall. Of course that only made my worst nightmares come true. The blade fell over and over again. I could always see it coming, but I couldn't stop it. Or so I thought.

What I took a long time to realise was that I was the one who was bringing all the pain on myself. It was me who continued to put my head down onto the block. If there was to be a change, I would have to make it happen myself. I couldn't stop the past from being with me, but I could stop it from controlling me.

I had to become courageous. I was still afraid of those feelings that turned my stomach and made me want to run as far away as I could go. But I had to stand firm and face them, and not let them rule my life. They're still there to this day, but I get by. Every now and then I feel the urge to destroy myself and the life I have made, but I sit with those feelings and breathe deep and the nightmares slowly pass.

By the way, I'm not telling you this for your benefit. I'm just reminding myself what to do. The past is always there, so I need to live in the moment.

# The Horse and Snail

As I've discovered, hospitals can be places of trauma and despair. But now and again they serve up lighter moments, whether it's due to the people, the circumstances or ... the drugs.

I've become more familiar than I'd really like to be with St Vincent's Private Hospital in Sydney, not just because I've had a few major operations there, but also because good friends keep ending up there too. One time, Jane's father, John Mahoney, was in for surgery. John is a good man. Salt of the earth, easy-going, straighty one-eighty. Given that he was also a career diplomat, I think it would be safe to say that he has not, at any stage of his life, been someone who would willingly partake in the use of drugs. There is a school of thought that says that if you can remember the 1960s, then you weren't there. John was definitely there and he remembers it all like it was yesterday. And that's despite the fact that at the height of the swinging sixties he was living in Rome, where I'm sure most people his age at some point tried a little puff of something to make the music sound funny. Not John. He had a job to do and a family to bring up. I'd guess that the wildest he ever got was having a few drinks on the terrace with visiting dignitaries.

Anyway, John had been in need of a hip replacement for a few years, but because of his age – eighty-seven – he'd been putting it off, thinking that it was too late to go through such an ordeal. But when I was having my hip surgery, I told Dr John Rooney, my friend and surgeon, about John and he said he was making a mistake.

'Jimmy,' he said, 'there's something we say about people like John.'

John and Phorn on their wedding day in December 1963. How lucky was I
to join their family?

'Oh yes. What's that?'

'Well, we don't say it to them directly because it sounds a bit callous, but it's true. We say that people John's age are hard to kill.'

'Really?'

'No, hear me out. They don't get to that age without being very tough. I think he should come in and let me have a good look at him and we'll see if he's all right to proceed.'

I took John in to see Dr Rooney and it was decided that rather than put up with his dodgy hip for the rest of his life he'd be better to go through the surgery and have a chance of being pain free for the foreseeable future – never for good, alas.

So we booked John in for the operation. But a few days before the scheduled date, he fell over and broke five ribs. It was serious, and he ended up at St Vincent's. By the time Jane went to visit him, he had been given so many drugs he was as high as a kite.

He wasn't making a lot of sense, so Jane sat by his bed, every now and again touching his hand reassuringly and telling him he was going to be all right. At one point a young nurse walked in to check his vitals. John lifted his head from the pillow and said, 'Hey, you. You can't bring that horse in here.'

Then he lay back down quietly.

I don't know if the nurse had big teeth or what, but I laughed about that for days.

A day or two later, during another of Jane's visits, John was watching a cricket match and he kept saying the bowlers were running off the television and onto his walls. 'Look, there they go again. Did you see that? They're running on the walls now. This is amazing television coverage!'

Well, I'm still not sure what they gave him, but whatever it was, it was working. Before long, he'd recovered from the broken ribs and was ready for his hip surgery.

I'm pleased to say that went well – and that once again his recovery provided some laughs, thanks to the same mix of anaesthetic and painkillers. When Jane and I went to take him some home-cooked food, he greeted us with, 'Ah. You're back, finally. I'm exhausted because of you two.'

We looked at each other, bewildered. 'What are you talking about, John?' I asked.

'You two took me out of the hospital last night,' he replied.

'Oh yes. And where did we go?'

'Well, I'm not sure, but we went across a lake on a multicoloured blanket thing that floated.'

'Okay …'

'Then you made me climb that mountain up to the cave.'

'All right then. And how did you go with that new hip you just got put in yesterday?'

'Oh, that was fine. But you made me go to sleep on the floor, in the dirt, and when I woke up I was here in this bloody big hotel with all these girls looking after me.'

'This is the hospital, John.'

'Well, it is now. But I tell you, last night it was a hotel.'

At this point I thought I'd let Jane feed her dad some nice food and I would take a walk to visit another old friend of mine who just happened to be in an adjacent ward, recovering from the same operation as John. Hip replacements are all the rage, apparently.

Glenn A. Baker is a rock historian, and over the years we have worked together on a lot of projects – it was Glenn who suggested that INXS and I record 'Good Times' by the Easybeats, a song that right to this day is a highlight in my set.

I wandered around until I found Glenn's room, knocked and walked in. In the far corner, Glenn was sitting in a chair. He looked fine, but as I spoke to him his eyes kept darting towards the door.

'Hey, Glenn. How are you holding up?'

'Yeah, Jimmy. I'm … I'm fine. Except for that giant snail that keeps climbing up the wall.'

He was staring over my shoulder and out into the corridor, nervously searching for the beast that he was sure was prowling the hallway. Glenn's a funny guy, and I thought for a while that he was kidding. My next thought was to go out and hire a giant snail suit and then walk around outside his door wearing a stethoscope. But I soon realised he was serious and that any jokes I made might push him over the edge.

'Okay then, Glenn. I'll see you later. Don't worry, mate, snails are so slow. If it comes back, just run to the nurses' station. It'll never catch you.'

I don't know what drugs they were giving these guys, but they didn't seem to be the ones I'd got during my recovery. I'm going to have to put in a special request next time I go in.

# A Walk on the Dark Side

Last time we were in Edinburgh, my nephew Paul decided it was time he went on a tourist outing with us. It ended up being an unnerving experience.

Paul had lived with us in Australia for a few years and, besides being our favourite Scottish nephew, had become as close to us as our kids. When he eventually left and went back to Scotland, he would phone us at all hours of the night and sing songs to us. Like clockwork, somewhere around midnight in Sydney every weekend, he would call after having a big night out that had run on into the next day in Glasgow. Paul didn't seem to sleep a lot on the weekends.

Jane and I would turn the light off and just be starting to drift into a deep sleep when – *ring-ring, ring-ring* – we'd be dragged back to reality by the noisy phone on the bedside table.

'Jimmy?' Jane would say.

'Huh?'

'Jimmy, wake up, it's Paul.'

'How do you know?'

'It's Paul, for sure.'

'Huh, what? It's your phone ringing, not mine.'

'Yes, it's my phone, but you know it's your nephew. He always calls at this time.'

'Ignore it and go back to sleep. I'll call him tomorrow.'

'But it might be serious, Jimmy. Maybe something's happened to him. You'd better answer it.' Jane had a soft spot for Paul.

'But it's your phone.'

'Jimmy!'

'Right, I've got it.'

I'd stagger out of bed, fall over shoes and clothing on Jane's side of the bed, then fumble for the phone in the dark – all so she could stay asleep.

'Ahem. Hello.'

Silence on the other end for about thirty seconds. Then I'd hear his voice. One fairly typical conversation went as follows.

'Is that ma Uncle Jimmy?'

'Yes, Paul, it's me.'

More silence, then it started. Loud and defiant but ever so teary and slightly slurred. I recognised the melody before I remembered the name of the song: 'Caledonia'. Paul sang those lyrics about how much he loved us and how he thinks about us all the time and how he was now going home. 'Come on, Jim. Sing it with me.'

'Paul, it's one in the morning here. Where are you?'

'I went out for a few drinks with ma pal after dinner last night, and we're still going.'

'You're in Glasgow then?'

'Nae fuckin' way. We caught the train down to London while we were drunk last night and now we've made it all the way tae Wales to see Tom Jones play at a festival today. It was great, so it was.'

'You went out for a drink in Glasgow and ended up at a Tom Jones show in Wales?'

'Aye, we did.'

I was wide awake now. This was a big night, even for Paul, and it was impressive even by his high standards. And I use the term *high* loosely.

'So, Paul, I thought you were getting healthy these days.'

'Aye, ah am. While am down here, am gonnae run in the London marathon tomorrow.'

'But you've been awake for two days already.'

'Aye, ah have. I don't think I'll win.'

I was stunned. 'How was Tom's show?'

'Aw, it was great, Jimmy, until they threw us oot.'

'What did they throw you out for?'

'Well, ye see, Jim, me and ma pal John ran doon the front and took off all our clathes and threw our underpants at Tom.'

'Well, I can see why he'd be angry.'

'Na, na, Jimmy. He loved us. He was laughing, so he was. His manager didnae like it though. So he chucked us oot. He said we were a distraction fae the audience. But, fuck, they were laughing along as well.'

'Paul, you're a madman, and I've got to get some sleep, so I can't talk anymore.'

'Aye, that's aw right. I didnae ring you anyway. I wanted tae talk to ma favourite aunty, Jane.'

I gently shook Jane. 'He wants *you*, Jane,' I whispered as I passed the phone to her. Then I drifted off to sleep to the sound of twenty great Scottish songs being sung ever so emotionally over the phone to Jane.

So, whenever we go to Scotland, we have to see Paul. We love him.

This time round, he was living in Edinburgh and had finally decided it was time to explore the city outside its pubs. 'Aye, Jim, let's see what happens in this toon after dark. I've lived on and off here fer years, so it'll be good to see what rubbish they tell the tourists. Probably a load of shite, but we'll wait and see, aw right?'

We booked a ghost tour that was scheduled to start as the sun went down. Our party included my daughter Eliza Jane, her fiancé, Jimmy, me and Paul – all ready to be scared out of our wits. (Jane had quickly volunteered to stay in our hotel to look after EJ and Jimmy's son, Teddy, figuring she'd have a lot more fun.) We were told to meet on the Royal Mile, just outside the old Tron Kirk. I'd read quite a few stories about that church and knew it was a spooky place to start.

Two other groups were waiting in the same place for their guides: a party of loudly dressed Scandinavians, standing politely and patiently, and a group of drunken Englishmen who were busy knocking back as much booze as they could before the start of the tour and offending anyone who came near them. I prayed we'd all keep well away from them as we waited.

Soon those groups wandered off with their respective guides – two clean-cut male students in casual clothes – but ours seemed to be late. As we waited, we joked about the upcoming tour.

'Ye know it'll be shite, Jim, don't ye,' said Paul, who for some reason was keen for us to be disappointed. Maybe because he'd been in Edinburgh for a while and didn't want to feel like he'd been missing out.

Time dragged on. Eventually, a rather striking woman approached us. Dressed in a full-length red gown and a small bonnet, she looked like an extra from *The Handmaid's Tale*.

'Good evening to you all,' she called out. 'My name is Esmerrrelda, and I hope you are rrrready to be terrrrrified. Because this town has a lot of darrrk secrrrets locked beneath the surface of its filthy strrreets. Ha ha ha ha!'

The other groups were well on their way and we had the end of the street almost to ourselves. The sun had gone down and the Royal Mile had suddenly taken on a ghostly glow. Our guide was an extremely pale young woman with thick, jet-black hair and a strong Eastern European accent. I wasn't sure if she was trying to sound like a vampire, or if that was her real voice. She would shout the start of each announcement then whisper the punch line, rolling her r's and simultaneously rolling her eyes when she wanted to heighten the drama of any particular statement.

I think she'd worked out that I was half deaf, because she'd begin talking softly, then as we moved closer she would suddenly shout and we would all jump back.

She knew we were a good audience. Even Paul had gone quiet.

We walked up the Royal Mile as our guide pointed out places of interest.

'This wall herrre is special. I need someone to help me tell this story now. Who will be my victim – oh, I mean my volunteer.' She scanned our faces. 'You!' she shouted.

Young Jimmy, Eliza-Jane's fiancé, had a look of terror on his face. Jimmy is a gentle, soft-spoken Kiwi fellow. Clearly the guide could tell just by looking at him that her delivery was having the desired effect. He was becoming quieter and more withdrawn every time we stopped, and every time she raised her voice he jumped into the air.

'Yes, you. The handsome, quiet one. Come to me and stand next to me.'

Jimmy reluctantly moved forward and stood by her side.

'Durrring the Rrreforrmation, this wall behind me was used to punish those who lied to the church. Blasphemers and sinners each one!'

She looked at Jimmy and gently stroked his face before roughly grabbing his hair and thrusting his head towards the wall.

'If the blasphemers were caught the prosecutors would drrrag them to this wall and … I would like you, handsome, to guess what they did next.'

Jimmy shuffled his feet and looked to me for help. I turned the other way, as if I'd suddenly spotted something of interest in the distance. He was on his own.

'Let me show you,' the guide continued. 'They would grrrrab a hammer, like this one.' Out of nowhere, as if by magic – though it could have been the light or our imaginations – what looked like a hammer appeared in her hand. 'And then they would nail theirrr tongues to the wall – like this!' *Bang!* She smashed the hammer against the stone wall right in front of Jimmy's face.

'Ha ha ha ha! But no, you would never do that. You would never lie to me, would you darrrling?'

She let go of his hair and once again slid her hand gently across his now pale Kiwi face. Jimmy it seemed, had escaped unhurt. But from then on he stood behind one of us, usually Eliza Jane, whenever we stopped, seeking protection from someone he was increasingly convinced was a witch.

Each stop brought increasingly terrifying tales of violence, torture and supernatural beings. It became clear that our guide had an extraordinary knowledge of Edinburgh's history.

As darkness enveloped the Old Town, we stopped at Greyfriars Kirkyard, the city's most famous cemetery, said to be one of the most haunted of all graveyards.

'If you look herrre at these grrraves,' our guide pointed out, 'you will see that they arrre coverrred in metal frrrames. What do you think these were for, my lovelies?'

I took an educated guess. 'To stop people stealing jewellery from the graves?'

'Ha, no!' she shouted, her face twisting and turning as she looked to the sky. I waited for a peal of thunder. But even this girl, as good as she was, couldn't organise that. 'You are wrrong! They did not want to steal the jewellery; they wanted to take dead bodies. Ha ha ha ha. Grave rrrrobberrs. They rrroamed the cemetery at night. Stealing the bodies for medical experiments! Soon people had to build these metal cages acrross the graves to stop them and others stealing bodies. If a family couldn't afford a cage for their rrrelative, they would sleep on the grrrave – until the body was too decomposed to be worth stealing.'

'Other crrriminals murrrdered people and sold their bodies to the universities. Two young Irishmen, William Burke and William Hare, killed sixteen people and sold their corpses to a prrrofessor of surrrgery and anatomy, Robert Knox, for dissecting and using in lectures. Ha ha ha!'

A carved gravestone in spooky Greyfriars Kirkyard. *(Shutterstock)*

I'd read something about this, but again she seemed to have in-depth, first-hand knowledge of the events and the crimes.

By now, we were ready to get the hell out of the cemetery and back to the relatively bright lights of the main street.

The final stop did us all in.

'Now, my lovelies, I will take you below the ground to the undergrrround catacombs, where even worse things happened.'

Jimmy was pale and ready to go home by this point, and Paul looked like he needed a drink. Our guide took us below the street, down three storeys, and with every step we took I could feel the hairs standing up on the back of my neck. At the bottom, she led us into an underground vault where tables and other furniture were scattered around. The air was damp and foul. Something about the place really scared me – you could sense that unspeakable acts had taken place there. I was on the point of making a dash for the exit. But I took a deep breath and soldiered on.

As we walked silently through the catacombs, the guide told us stories of hundreds of children with the plague being brought down here and left to die. Locked in these very rooms alone until they passed away. Her description, and the silence, made me feel sick. Now I had to get to the surface. Fortunately, it was the end of the visit, but as we climbed back up the stairs, I pushed my way past our guide and ran all the way to the street.

As we gathered on the pavement, catching our breath, none of us could speak. We eyed our guide with fear and suspicion.

Instead of scowling back at us, she smiled demurely and said, 'Well, thank you for taking my tour, and I hope you have a great time here in Edinburgh.' She still sounded Eastern European, but she was no longer rolling her r's quite as much.

Still smiling, she flicked back her jet-black locks, backed slowly into the shadows of a dark, damp alley – and was gone.

We followed Paul to the nearest pub and drank straight whiskies in silence. You could see everyone's brain working overtime. How come our guide had been dressed in clothes of the period, while the others wore modern dress? How did she manage to appear from nowhere, and vanish just as suddenly? Where had that hammer come from? And how did she know so much about the witch trials and the grave-robbing – every tiny gory detail – and seem to feel the pain of those events so acutely? Was she really a guide – or something else entirely?

# Scot Rock

| | |
|---:|:---|
| 'Jealous Guy' | FRANKIE MILLER |
| 'The Faith Healer' | THE SENSATIONAL ALEX HARVEY BAND |
| 'Reflections of My Life' | MARMALADE |
| 'Rocks' | PRIMAL SCREAM |
| 'The American' | SIMPLE MINDS |
| 'I'm Gonna Be (500 Miles)' | THE PROCLAIMERS |
| 'No More "I Love You's"' | ANNIE LENNOX |
| 'Take Me Out' | FRANZ FERDINAND |
| 'Someone You Loved' | LEWIS CAPALDI |
| 'Wishing Well' | MAGGIE BELL |
| 'Stupid Girl' | GARBAGE |
| 'Pick Up the Pieces' | AVERAGE WHITE BAND |
| 'Baker Street' | GERRY RAFFERTY |
| 'Caledonia' | FRANKIE MILLER |
| 'To Sir with Love' | LULU |
| 'Going Home' (theme to *Local Hero*) | MARK KNOPFLER |
| 'I Don't Want A Lover' | TEXAS |

# An Absolute Steal

I know a lot of car salesmen who are really good people, but there must be a reason they are often spoken about in such derogatory terms.

People say, *Don't trust him, he's a real car salesman*. Or, *Would you buy a used car from a man like him?* At social gatherings I've heard car salesmen called 'untrustworthy', 'annoying', 'sleazy', 'slimy' and 'manipulative', and that was by their good friends. I guess all it takes is a few shysters for them to get a bad name.

Now, I'm not a suspicious soul. I have faith in people's goodwill. You might even call me gullible – I know that Jane does. I tend to believe all that I am told. For example, I once had a surgeon tell me he'd need to bolt my back together with metal rods or I'd collapse and die. That seemed a bit drastic and I wasn't sure I was ready for such treatment, but I thought I'd better do as I was told. Then, only a few days before the scheduled procedure, Jane wondered if we should get a second opinion.

The second doctor told me, to my great relief, that I didn't need to go that far. 'Your back is not good, but you're not quite ready for that procedure yet,' he said. 'Put it off for as long as you possibly can.'

I pointed out that the first doctor was one of the most highly regarded surgeons in the country. 'I mean, he's done surgery on some really famous Australians, for fuck's sake.'

'Oh, him,' the second doctor shot back. 'That's just his way. Don't listen to him.'

So, if you can't trust a revered doctor, why would you ever trust a used car salesman.

With any goods you buy, it pays to listen to what sales staff have to say and then shop around. And especially when it comes to something you'll be driving and moving your children around in at high speed. Right?

I wasn't always so wise. At one point back in the early 1980s, I wanted to buy a car for Jane for her birthday. By that time, I had made some decent money, though not a fortune. This was when we were living at Mount Gibraltar in the Southern Highlands, about 120 kilometres from Sydney, so we needed a good, trustworthy car that would get us to and from the city safely. I knew that 3 Series BMWs were really well made, and if the mileage was low enough the car would run for as long as we needed it to. So I started looking for a good second-hand one, something in great condition.

A friend recommended a dealer in the Wollongong area and assured me that he could be trusted. 'Listen, Jimmy,' he warned me, 'there are some real lowlife, scumbag sharks out there, and I would hate for you to be taken advantage of. Ring this guy. His name is Dominic. He'll look after you. He's been in the business for a long, long time. Christ, he even sold me that last Holden ute I bought.'

'You mean the one that burst into flames on the freeway while you were driving at a hundred and twenty kilometres an hour with the kids in the car?'

'Yep, that's the guy. But it wasn't his fault. He told me that his mechanic was a crook and had been using cheap electrical parts he'd imported from behind the Iron Curtain. It's still a good car. I mean, you can hardly see the marks left by the flames. In fact, he thanked me for bringing it to his notice. He's a good guy.'

I know. That should have been enough to warn me off. But no, I took his advice and made the call to the car yard.

'Hi, is that Dominic? Look, it's Jimmy Barnes here. Yes, that's right, the singer. No, not Midnight Oil, that's Peter Garrett. Cold Chisel. Yes, that's right, the band that sang "Ita", yes. Glad you like it.'

I wanted to tell him that 'Ita' was a bit of a joke song and definitely not one of our best, but it wasn't my job to judge his musical taste. I just hoped his knowledge of cars was more extensive than his knowledge of music.

'Great, what can I do you for?' he asked enthusiastically. 'I mean do for you.'

Even though I thought I could hear him rubbing his hands together and trying not to laugh, I explained what I thought I needed.

He had a whole spiel ready. 'Mate, you are so lucky. I've got this car here that was just traded in yesterday and is an absolute steal. The old lady who owned it never drove above eighty kilometres an hour. It's spent most of its life sitting outside the Wollongong Ladies' Knitting Club covered in plastic to protect it from the elements. In fact, it's been driven so little that it still has the original tyres on it. That car has been serviced by our company since the day it was manufactured and I've got all the hand-written log books – in fact, they are here drying on my desk as we speak. Ha ha, only kidding, mate, this car is immaculate.'

He took a quick breath. 'If you give me a day or two I'll bang some wider wheels on it – I know you music people like things to look snazzy – and get it detailed. And, I shouldn't be saying this, but, what the hell, I love your music, I've always loved the Oils, so I'll even slip in a new stereo, some speakers and a subwoofer that'll burst your eardrums, and send it up for a test drive. Promise me you won't tell my boss or you'll get me sacked. Now, to be straight up with you, because I'm an honest man, I've got to let you know, there are quite a few other people interested in purchasing this vehicle. So if you really want it, let me know ASAP. But no pressure.'

I explained how much I wanted to spend.

'Jesus, you make it tough on a guy,' he responded, 'but I tell you what I'm going to do – and you have to promise me you'll keep this to yourself. I'll fix the tyres and the stereo and, fuck it, I'll tint the windows real dark, you know, pimp it up a bit, all at my own expense, just because I like you, and I'll give it to you for – I can't believe I'm doing this! – I'll give it to you for forty-five thousand dollars. There you go, I've said it now, so I can't take it back. Do we have a deal?'

Even I wasn't that stupid. I knew he'd charge extra for the tint somewhere down the line. That stuff's not cheap.

'If the car's good, I'll take it,' I said decisively. 'Send it up.'

I hung up the phone and was suddenly overcome by the urge to have a long, hot shower.

That afternoon a cute little blue-grey 3 Series BMW pulled into the driveway while Jane was out shopping. Dominic had brought the car to the house himself, with his offsider following, to drive him home. I knew it was him as soon as he got out of the car. His suit was ill-fitting and a little bit dirty, his eyes were very close together, and he kept shuffling his feet. I noticed he couldn't look me in the eye.

'There she is,' he announced. 'What a beauty. You drive it around this evening and we can sign all the papers tomorrow.'

He left and I took the car for a spin. Even though I knew he was probably a crook, the car was surprisingly good. I decided to keep it, and as soon as I got to the house I went inside and surprised Jane with the keys.

When she saw the car, she was initially thrilled, and she walked round it, running her hands along the immaculate paintwork, and sat in the driver's seat, checking the controls and admiring the leather seats. But as she climbed out of the car, a shadow passed over her face and she asked, 'How much did you pay, Jimmy?'

Jane was always worried that people took advantage of me.

'Jane, it was a steal. It only cost forty-five thousand dollars. And the guy has assured me that if we don't like it, he'll buy it back from me tomorrow for more than we paid for it. How good a deal is that?'

Jane looked at me sceptically, then her excitement got the better of her and she hopped back in the car and took it for a drive.

On her return, she hugged me and told me she loved the car. 'I'm so glad that he didn't take advantage of you,' she said. 'You really should have let me deal with him, though. You know that those second-hand car dealers would steal from their own mothers, and you are just too nice.'

That night I slept like a baby, happy in the knowledge that I had made a good deal and got a great car for Jane. I woke up early the next day and stepped out of the house to greet the morning. There in the driveway was the new car, looking magnificent as the rising sun shone down on the frost that covered every surface. I walked around my new investment just to take it all in.

Then something caught my eye. Outlined in the ice on the front windscreen, in big numbers, was the price that had been on the car while it sat in the yard: twenty-five thousand dollars.

I calmly walked into the kitchen and picked up the phone to call my new friend before Jane got out of bed. He didn't answer, so I left a very clear message.

'Dominic, Jimmy Barnes from Mental as Anything here. I just read the real price of the car on the windscreen. I need you to come and take it off my property – before I set fire to it.'

# The Singer and the Superstar

The singer walked up the winding driveway, past the limousines and their chauffeurs, and climbed the steps to the sumptuous restaurant overlooking the bay.

He found his table and sat in his designated seat. It was no accident that he'd been placed directly across from the international superstar – he was here for a reason, after all. As a favour. Certainly not by choice.

The superstar was gaunt and pale, not in a healthy way but in a tortured, painful way. His concave cheeks looked like oyster shells that had been shucked and emptied, and his face seemed to be caving in as a result of years of denying himself anything that contained the slightest traces of sugar or, heaven forbid, animal fat. His eyes were cold and his hair stood straight up as if trying to flee from the rest of his body. His limbs were long and lean – too long and lean for his own good. They would have been at home on the body of a Russian ballet dancer, but on him they looked ridiculous. Stretching out from his scrawny British body that, no matter how much exercise he did, would never change, they appeared gangly and awkward, as if God had taken them out of the wrong box.

His clothes, though, were immaculate, and had been chosen no doubt by the outrageously expensive stylist who dressed him as he travelled the world: linen trousers, stylishly too short and perfect for showing off the Om tattoo on his ankle; Italian slip-on calf-leather shoes that probably cost more than the singer's car; and a white silk shirt that hung from his shoulders and clung to his suntanned arms. He'd never really worked a day in his life – he was a natural-born superstar after all. In fact the last real 'job' he'd had was as a school prefect back at the sprawling country school that occupied half of the county where he grew up in rural England. His childhood had been perfect and now his career was too.

The singer, deafened by years of working in factories and relentless blaring guitar solos in overcrowded clubs, struggled to hear the conversations across the table. He could only pick up the odd word here and there. Most of what was being said meant nothing to him, but he caught enough of it to know he wasn't really interested anyway.

'Blah blah blah … I like playing the Macedonian bouzouki … Yabba yabba yabba … I adore my German tantric Pilates classes. I have them every day in my private jet. It's ever so satisfying. I can do it for hours on end now – the bouzouki playing, that is.' He broke out in a low, lecherous laugh.

'What am I doing here?' wondered the singer, still dusty from the previous night's revelries. His mind drifted off as the first course, lobster smothered in sea urchin sauce, was served. He searched the flowers that decorated the table for somewhere to hide his slimy, untouched plateful. It was going to be a long afternoon.

He was only there because the previous day his dear friend, a beautiful, self-made millionaire, shameless self-promoting music mogul and part-time female Svengali, had begged him to attend the lunch. They had been partners in crime for years, been through good times and bad together, and had always had each other's backs. She knew all too well that the singer would do anything for her.

'You'll love it,' she'd told him. 'The best in the business will be at the table. And you know what to say to these people. You're practically one of them.'

The singer knew she mainly wanted him there as support: she had plans for the evening that would most certainly mean she would be way too hungover on the following day to look after anyone at the lunch but herself.

'Besides, it'll be good for your career.'

The singer had cringed uncomfortably when he heard this. He knew she believed he was no longer at the top of his game but didn't have the heart to tell him. Clearly she thought she might as well get some use out of him while she still could.

Now here he was, feeling like a fish out of water — which, unsurprisingly, turned out to be the next course in this lunch, the most torturous experience he'd had since he'd last eaten at that same Melbourne restaurant.

All at once, the superstar, obviously being ever so entertained by a glamorously dressed older woman to the left of him — the partner of the music mogul — threw his head back and emitted a booming laugh that carried down the table, bounced off the perfectly polished glass doors that opened out onto Port Phillip Bay, and rattled the cutlery. It was as if he wanted the world, or at least the rest of the table, to know how deeply connected with his host and her partner he really was. He was a man of the people after all.

Despite his fine upbringing, he'd cut his teeth in the music industry wearing torn clothes held together by safety pins and playing in a punk band that bridged the class barrier and made it possible for middle-class music lovers to feel that they too were part of the angry working-class music revolution. Even though, if the truth be known, the revolution had already come and gone while the superstar was busy spending his daddy's money on the French Riviera on yet another gap year – five years after leaving school.

The singer sensed a lull in the conversation and prepared to tackle the job he had been given: strike up a conversation that would break the ice with the superstar, who, at all costs, according to the millionaire music mogul, had to be made to feel comfortable and loved. His chance came as the superstar's eyes alighted on the singer's for a fleeting second. But before the humble singer could open his mouth, those piercing eyes moved on, looking for someone more important and more deserving of his precious time.

To the right of the superstar sat a man who was obviously a film director. It was obvious because he had announced it many times to the table. Now he was saying to the middle-aged woman next to him, 'You know I am a vegan, right. On my movie sets we don't serve any animal products like these.' He scoffed at the ridiculously expensive seafood that now covered the table. 'There are no animals allowed on my set but me, darling. That's why I'm on a carefully selected diet today, you see. Everyone knows that I am strictly vegan. Actually, that would be a good name for my next film, *Strictly Vegan*.' He turned to the young buffed boy with bulging biceps crouching behind him – who looked like he had an IQ not much higher than his age and was no doubt paid a pittance to follow him around and write down all the wonderful things that oozed from his mouth – and said, 'Write that down.'

Clearly desperate to establish some sort of connection with someone, anyone, he spoke way too loudly. It seemed everyone at the table did. It was as if they were used to people never standing close enough to them to use a normal conversational tone. Everything they said sounded like an order, barked out in the manner of a sergeant major, requiring someone to jump or, at the very least, gush with enthusiasm.

'Maybe you could help me with some music for my next little film,' the director hissed as he slid closer to the touring superstar.

The room began to buzz. Everyone at the table seemed excited by the prospect of a collaboration being arranged right then and there, in front of their very eyes.

'Someone should be filming this!' shouted an over-excited personal assistant from the end of the table, far from where the real guests were seated – so far that no one who mattered paid him any attention anyway.

The singer noticed a slight taste of vomit had just risen from his turning stomach to his mouth. He picked up his glass of mineral water – it came from a glacier on the South Island of New Zealand and had been imported by their host especially for the occasion – and gargled loudly. All the guests fell silent for a moment, then, as quickly as they'd stopped, went back to their gossip and continued to ignore him all over again.

The superstar's eyes once again met the singer's. Maybe it was out of curiosity, or perhaps sheer disgust. Whatever the reason, his glance lingered just long enough for the singer to initiate a conversation.

'So, how are you enjoying our beautiful country then?'

The superstar looked at him thoughtfully for a second and tilted his head slightly as if he was thinking of a deep and meaningful answer to the challenging question the singer had just posed him. Then he turned and continued talking to the film director, completely ignoring the singer.

'Well,' thought the singer, 'I guess my work here is done. Either that or he doesn't speak English.' He picked up his phone and car keys and dropped them into his jacket pocket. 'Maybe one day I'll be famous enough to ignore normal people, and pay someone to gather my things for me.'

Without anyone noticing, he stepped away from the table, then walked around to where the superstar was seated. He leaned down and spoke into his ear. 'Not sure anyone has told you this lately, but you really are a pompous, pretentious, poncy prick of a person. And, by the way, your fly has been undone since you walked into the room. Love your work!'

He turned and headed towards the music mogul, who sat a few seats down from the superstar, nervously sipping her champagne and repeatedly scanning the room to check every detail of the goings-on. She was oblivious to the spanner the singer had just thrown in the works.

He kissed her gently on the cheek and smiled. 'I think we have that all sorted out now, so I'm off. Any problems, just give me a call.

As he walked slowly down the winding driveway towards his car parked under a tree out on the street, he experienced a strange sense of achievement. Reaching his vehicle, he looked at the white marks splashed across the windscreen, courtesy of the hundreds of well-fed birds that lived in the trees of this leafy, up-market, ridiculously expensive part of the city, and laughed.

Climbing into his wreck of a car, which he had paid for with his own hard-earned money, he felt he was back where he belonged, and as he turned on the windscreen wipers, he allowed himself another little chuckle of satisfaction. Despite all he had just experienced, he could still see through the shit.

He loved the rock 'n' roll business.

# A Unifying Sound

'Hey, Ian, you want to hear some music, mate?' Ian Moss slowly turned his head and looked at me long and hard.

He was driving us from Melbourne on a seemingly endless road to our next gig, at the Bondi Lifesaver in Sydney. Three different states in as many days. We were running on adrenaline and enthusiasm and anything else we could get our hands on.

Ian's eyes were bloodshot and seemed to have sunk back into his head.

'Hey, Ian. Ahem … Ian, the road.'

'What? Wh—'

'The road!' I screamed.

'Where?'

'The one right in front of you. Look at the road, mate, not me. You can talk to me without looking.'

'Yeah, that's a good idea.' He swung his head back to face forwards and peered into the darkness.

We both laughed uncomfortably. Poor Ian had been very keen to drive when he was full of steam after the gig, but that steam was rapidly disappearing.

'Glad we've got that settled. Now, do you want some music?'

'Yeah, that'd be great, mate …'

In the late seventies, Cold Chisel liked to drive everywhere. Well, when I say we liked to drive, we really didn't have a choice. We used to play in towns so small that you couldn't fly to them unless you were in a crop duster, so it was either drive or walk. In the first few years there were times when all we could really afford to do was walk, and occasionally, when our bank account was empty, we would have to hitchhike. But somehow we'd usually manage to scrounge an advance from a dodgy manager or find an agent who felt sorry for us and scrape together enough cash to rent a station wagon.

No doubt it was all character-building and good for the music. I'm sure Don Walker wrote some of his best songs while standing on the side of an endless highway in the middle of the night, being eaten alive by mosquitos while trucks barrelled past him at 120 kilometres an hour, sounding their horns and giving him the finger. You don't think 'Houndog' came to him after a short hop on a Learjet nibbling on crackers and caviar and sipping champagne, do you? No, going on the road has inspired some of the best rock 'n' roll songs ever written. Good rock tunes don't happen if you are too comfortable. You need to be hungry, lean and mean and looking for a way out of the deep shit you might be in.

After a few years of driving cheap rental cars, we finally started pulling enough people to our shows to look at other options. For a while we drove a little minibus with terrible seats and just enough room above the luggage in the back to lie flat on your back, with your nose nearly touching the roof, and sleep. But there was always a chance that whoever was driving would need to slam on the brakes and you might wake up flying through the air before smashing into any of the band members who happened to be still sitting up, staring out the windows. Not a pleasant experience, and in the end the bus had to go.

At the height of our success we bought a mustard-coloured, long-wheelbase LandCruiser with roof racks big enough to fit most of our luggage – the rest lay around our feet. The mustard colour made us less obvious to the few fans who'd started following us, and to the local police who might be looking for a chance to run us out of town. No one, not even the police, thought that a supposedly cool rock band would be seen dead in a car that colour, and they were right: we weren't very cool.

We fitted the LandCruiser out with Recaro seats so we'd be safe and comfortable, and a sound system that was loud enough to drown out the ice-cold silence on those nights when we weren't talking to each other. You see, contrary to popular belief, the members of Cold Chisel didn't always get on. In fact, sometimes we wanted to kill each other. It was funny that the same thing that stopped us getting signed to any record label in their right mind when we were young and hungry ended up being the same thing that made us a great band. The tension between us was our secret weapon. If it erupted on stage, it made for an exciting show for the audience, but it could also happen in the studio or even in the car somewhere on the Hume Highway, racing to Sydney, late for a show. Our band was made up of five guys, each with an idea of how they wanted the band to sound. Some wanted it to be smooth. Some wanted it to be bluesy and some wanted to pin the audience to the back of the room and throttle them one by one. The one who could hold his nerve the longest or get the others on his side normally got his way. That is until we went on stage. Then all bets were off and I did whatever I wanted to do.

The choice of music played in our vehicle reflected that very same tension. Ian usually wanted to listen to something that displayed great skill and technique, like jazz supremo Larry Carlton. I'd have preferred to stick pins in my eyes and throw myself out of the moving car. Steve liked Stevie Wonder – melodic, cool music with very few guitars in the mix, which made me want to stand on top of the car and surf while it was being played. Don favoured Thelonious Monk. I didn't know what that was, so I never knew how to react to his request. Phil usually asked for the Paul Butterfield Blues Band or something similar, but he was so nice he wouldn't fight with any of us, so it was never played. I liked music to suit my mood, which in those days was always agitated and on the edge of going crazy. Funnily enough, I seemed to get my way a lot of the time, and before long the poor band were very sick of me and my music selection. I'm sure they would have preferred it if I had been standing on the roof of the car.

On this particular night, as we'd left a show at one of the many sweaty pubs we played in Melbourne, a punter had grabbed the collar of my leather jacket and slipped a cassette into my hand. 'Hey, Jimmy, why don't you have a listen to this?' he said. 'This is the best rock 'n' roll album ever.'

I grabbed the cassette and stepped a little closer to him, but he ducked and vanished from my field of vision before I could get a good swing at him. I was left standing alone outside our dirty mustard LandCruiser holding a tape I didn't really want, waiting for the band.

I knew for certain that I wasn't going to get much sleep, so I decided to sit up front with Ian and keep him company as he drove. But first I had to hide his Larry Carlton tape. As I jumped into the car and Ian was placing his bag on the roof, I slipped it under my legs and out of sight.

After jostling for their favourite seats, the boys were finally comfortable and we hit the road. It wasn't long until the band were sleeping like babies in the back, leaving Ian and me in silence in the front two seats. After an hour, Ian's eyes started looking heavy and I could see he wanted me to take over the driving. But I was in no condition to drive and knew nobody really wanted me to drive, because I drive like I sing: hard and fast. So that's when I suggested playing some music.

Having got the LandCruiser under control once more, Ian started glancing around and searching with his left hand. 'There's a Larry Carlton cassette somewhere around here. I left it on the seat so I could find it for the drive.'

'Oh shit,' I said, 'was that yours? I saw it sitting on the table in the dressing room. I thought it must have belonged to some other guitar nerd. But you must have left it behind.'

With my left hand I slipped his cassette out from under my legs and into my leather jacket pocket. I could dispose of it later when I found a rubbish bin. With my right hand, I banged my newly acquired cassette into the tape player before Ian could object. Written on the side of the cassette in biro was the name *Johnny Burnette and the Rock 'n Roll Trio*. I'd heard of them but didn't know their music. How bad could it be? Anything had to be better than Larry Carlton.

I cranked up the volume, sat back and waited. The music started, and from the opening bars of the first song I was dancing in my seat. If you've seen me dance, you'll know it's not pretty. That alone was probably enough to keep Ian awake for the next few hours.

Johnny Burnette and the Rock 'n Roll Trio. *(Getty Images)*

Very quickly, that tape became my favourite tape. I played it constantly in the car and I took it to parties and put it on whenever I could. And, amazingly, the whole band loved it, at least long enough to become fans of Johnny Burnette and the Rock 'n Roll Trio and their 'rockabilly' style.

I read up on my favourite new music and became fascinated by its origins and its links to my own Scottish heritage. Rock 'n' roll had of course developed initially in the southern United States, forming from a mixture of jazz and gospel music from southern churches. That rock 'n' roll was something we all appreciated and it had diversified into the range of rock styles that sometimes separated us. But at some point early rock 'n' roll music had also mixed with traditional music brought to America by Scottish and northern Irish immigrants in the early 1700s, many of whom settled in the Appalachian and Ozark mountains. Most of those immigrants were Protestants fleeing Catholic persecution in the early eighteenth century, and many of their songs celebrated Prince William of Orange, who had defeated the Catholic king James II at the Battle of the Boyne in Ireland in 1690. Consequently, they were referred to generally as 'Orangemen' or 'Billy Boys' and those who settled in the mountains became known as 'hillbillies'. And when these white trash from the country married their music with rock 'n' roll, the blend became known as 'rockabilly'.

It's a music that's raucous and wild, and as such it had appealed to me from the first time I heard it. Plus it was basically Scottish, so I was genetically attracted to it. Songs like Eddie Cochran's 'Somethin' Else' and Gene Vincent's 'Be-Bop-a-Lula' sounded great to me as a young boy listening to the radio, though I didn't know why. But then that style of music got lost in an onslaught of new sounds that constantly poured out of the radio in the sixties. I soon moved on to bands like The Beatles and The Rolling Stones, before the wildness of psychedelic music flooded my brain completely. Jimi Hendrix changed everything for me. From then on guitars had to be loud and distorted, and the cleaner, mono sounds of the fifties were forgotten.

So I'd long since stopped listening to rockabilly music until that cassette turned up in my hands. But as soon as it was played in the car that night I was once again drawn to it. I started hunting down old songs I'd heard as a child and looking for ways to bring that energy and spirit into our band. The songs I wrote in that style were the start of a long journey. 'Goodbye Astrid' was followed by 'Rising Sun' and 'You've Got Nothing I Want'. I wanted to write rebellious songs that lifted the tempo of our set and the spirits of our audiences. Producing songs that made people want to tear the walls down, that was my job in the band.

The other members of the band could see what I was trying to do and drove themselves harder and faster too. Rockabilly became a unifying sound that tied our diverse musical interests together. In the years that followed, Chisel delved deeper and deeper into rockabilly and 1950s rock 'n' roll. Don wrote songs with the same attitude, which soon became the sound that would define Cold Chisel.

I remember, many years later, Don telling a DJ somewhere in Europe that we loved rock 'n' roll. Trying to impress us, the DJ played a Guns N' Roses track.

'You know, mate,' Don said, 'this is not rock 'n' roll. It doesn't roll; in fact, I'm not sure it even rocks. We like real rock 'n' roll – Little Richard and Jerry Lee Lewis, that sort of thing. You get what I'm saying?'

Rockabilly music wasn't just a fad for us; it had been there from the beginning, before we even recognised what it was, and it is still an integral part of Cold Chisel's music. Whenever we get back together, it's evident. 'Rising Sun' and 'Don't Let Go' are not the only traces of rockabilly in our set. 'HQ454 Monroe' and 'No Plans' are both big rockabilly-influenced songs from our later albums that still feature heavily in our live show.

It seems the older we get and the more we look back, the more we draw from the music we grew up on. The older I get, the more I want to sound like Little Richard, screaming and distorting the microphones. The longer we play, the more Don tends to play piano like Jerry Lee Lewis – I half expect to look over and catch him playing with his feet. Charley Drayton, our 'new drummer' – we call him that even though he's played with us for more than ten years – plays rockabilly shuffles as well as anyone in the world. Ian is more often than not playing twangy reverb sounds on his old Gretsch guitar just like the rockabilly legends of days gone by. And if we could get Phil onto a double bass, we would all be jumping off the drum risers into the crowd and tearing it up.

Through my solo career and tours with my own band, the rockabilly influence loomed large too. In 1990, chart-topping rockabilly revivalists the Stray Cats toured Australia with me, which was the beginning of a long association. I recorded with Brian Setzer from the Stray Cats a number of times – you can find him playing low-down guitar on 'Little Darling' and bone-rattling riffs on 'Lay Down Your Guns'. The first record I made in America, *For the Working Class Man*, featured Billy Burnette, the nephew of Johnny Burnette, the band leader of the great Rock 'n Roll Trio that featured on the very cassette that was handed to me at that gig so many years ago.

Though I don't remember this, my dear friend Chris Cheney from The Living End told me recently that he came to see one of my solo shows at Festival Hall in Melbourne in the early nineties and gave me a cassette of his band playing, hoping we might get the chance to work together. He apparently looked very baby-faced and reckons I might not have taken him seriously. I think he may have already made a similar pitch to Slim Jim Phantom during the earlier tour. I'm not sure if Slim Jim remembers that fresh-faced young lad either. But if we'd paid attention and listened to Chris's tape, we all might have worked together much earlier than when we did.

Fast-forward thirty years and Chris, Slim Jim and I decided we finally had to put a band together. We needed a piano player, and with the help of Kevin Shirley, one of the greatest producers on the planet, we ended up getting together with the legendary Jools Holland and forming The Barnestormers. In 2023, we released a great rockabilly album. We even had a biplane on the cover.

The big lesson I learned from this whole story is never underestimate anyone who is passionate about music or you might just miss out on something great. It's funny how life offers so many opportunities, so many different roads to travel. You just have to be brave enough to take a deep breath and follow the ones that entice you.

We've still got big plans for The Barnestormers. I might just go out and buy myself a crop duster in case we ever want to tour rural Australia. I know those planes are only two-seaters and a little snug. And, yes, they are gas guzzlers. Not to mention there's little room for luggage. But it would be a great way to get some fresh air into your lungs before a show. Chris and I could always stand on the wings. I love a big entrance.

# Rockabilly Rhythms

| | |
|---|---|
| *Greatest Hits* (whole album) | JOHNNY BURNETTE AND THE ROCK 'N ROLL TRIO |
| 'Rock Around the Clock' | BILL HALEY AND HIS COMETS |
| 'Long Tall Sally' | LITTLE RICHARD |
| 'C'mon Everybody' | EDDIE COCHRAN |
| 'That'll Be the Day' | BUDDY HOLLY & THE CRICKETS |
| 'Folsom Prison Blues' | JOHNNY CASH |
| 'Blue Suede Shoes' | ELVIS PRESLEY |
| 'Twenty Flight Rock' | EDDIE COCHRAN |
| 'Be Bop a Lula' | GENE VINCENT |
| 'Red Hot' | BILLY LEE RILEY |
| 'Rising Sun' | COLD CHISEL |
| 'Chantilly Lace' | THE BIG BOPPER |
| 'Tutti Frutti' | LITTLE RICHARD |
| 'Somethin' Else' | EDDIE COCHRAN |
| 'Don't Let Go' | COLD CHISEL |
| 'Stray Cat Strut' | STRAY CATS |
| 'Sweet Love on My Mind' | THE BARNESTORMERS |

# For Whom the Bell Tolls

Fire alarms are of course lifesaving devices. Trouble is, I've heard so many go off for no good reason that I find myself hardly listening to them anymore.

It's like the boy who cried wolf for me. The fact I think this way clearly puts my own life at risk, so part of the reason I'm recounting the following stories is to remind myself to take fire alarms more seriously.

Nearly forty years ago we went to Hawaii to stay with Jane's parents. Her mum and dad, Phorn and John, had rented a huge apartment, twenty-six floors up in a high-rise apartment block near Waikiki, which looked out across the ocean. Each day we would wake up and swim in the glorious Pacific Ocean and then settle in for a day of reading or relaxing on the balcony while watching the sea. It was a beautiful place to unwind – until the day the fire alarm went off.

It was the hottest time of the day, when the last thing anybody wanted was to have to run down twenty-six flights of steps. But that was exactly what we were supposed to do when the bells and sirens started ringing, so loudly that it was impossible to ignore them.

It was my first fire emergency, so I was ready by the door with my backpack filled with passports and wallets before you could say 'towering inferno'. I'd even slipped in a bit of food and water in case we got trapped somewhere. None of the others had yet moved. Slowly, John and Jane wandered over to the door. Being a stickler for following the right procedures, John had read the fire-drill leaflet and knew exactly what we should be doing and where we should be doing it. Jane's mum, however, didn't seem to want to move at all.

'Right, everybody over here,' said John. 'We have to follow the arrows on the walls to the stairwell.'

I immediately thought, 'There are arrows on the walls? I've walked up and down this corridor a hundred times and I've never noticed them. If we can still see the arrows, then there's no smoke, so there can't be any fire either.'

'Over here, Mother.' That was what John lovingly called Jane's mum: Mother. 'It's time to move, and move quick.'

Phorn was still sitting on the couch, ignoring the noise and thumbing her way casually through a *Vogue* magazine. 'Oh, I think I'll just stay here, John,' she replied. 'I'll be all right. You can play your little fire-drill game. I'll still be here when you come back.'

But John was getting anxious. 'Look, Mother, this is not a game. If it was a drill, they would have notified us that it was happening. This is serious.'

'Yes, all right. But I'm staying here.'

I thought John might have a point. Maybe there was no smoke yet because we were so high up. The fire could have been far below. I ran to the balcony and looked down. I couldn't see smoke or flames, or smell smoke for that matter, but the hotel might have been completely ablaze around the other side. It was a long way to jump. I began to panic and ran back to the door. Phorn hadn't moved.

'Come on, Mum, you don't want to be trapped up here if there is a fire,' Jane said, trying to reason with her.

People from the other apartments on our floor were rushing down the corridor and into the stairwell, some of them screaming by this point. But Phorn wasn't going anywhere fast.

'You are going to have to move, Mother. This is not funny,' said John, trying his best not to raise his voice. He didn't want anyone to panic, but the three of us were by now standing outside the door.

Finally, Phorn relented. 'I'll come, but it's so stupid. There is no fire. Can anybody smell smoke?' Slowly, she walked out the door. She refused to move fast, as that would have been undignified.

I, on the other hand, had already run to the fireproof stairwell door and back about five times.

Jane could see the fear on my face. 'Come on, Mum,' she urged, 'we have to move quicker. It's an emergency. Look at Jimmy, he's scared.'

'All right, darling,' Phorn responded, unmoved, 'if you say so.' She smiled at Jane and sped up to a slow stroll. I'd seen people moving faster while window-shopping on Rodeo Drive, but at least she was moving.

In the stairwell people were walking in single file down the hundreds of stairs and staying generally calm, though a few extremely nervous residents ran past, pushing and screaming as though the fire was already licking at their feet. One or two slipped and fell, picked themselves up, saw their bleeding knees and shrieked even more, before continuing to hobble down the dozens of floors below them.

Clutching her handbag tightly as though it held the crown jewels, Phorn descended steadily, in an unruffled, leisurely fashion, not breaking a sweat. But about halfway down the stairs, she started laughing out loud. 'This is so stupid. We should go back now, John.'

'Don't be silly, Mother, we're going all the way down. We've got to get out of here.'

Her laugh was so infectious that we all started laughing too. Which only served to slow us all down. Soon total strangers who up to then had been terrified were laughing along with Jane's mum as well.

Then, abruptly, Phorn stopped laughing, turned around and headed back up the stairs, clearly all at once a woman with a mission. By this time the fire alarms seemed to be even louder than when we'd first started our descent.

'Where the hell are you going now, Mother?' John shrieked. He had to shout because she was already halfway up the first flight of stairs.

'I need to go back,' she called over her shoulder. 'I've left something behind.'

'Oh God, leave it, Phorn. Just leave it!' John was so agitated that he'd started using her real name in an attempt to get her to listen to reason. But it was no good and she disappeared up the next flight of stairs.

Jane turned to John and said, 'I'll go and get her. You keep going.'

As she sped off, I turned to John and said, 'I'll go and get them. You just keep moving,' and followed quickly behind Jane.

I have a picture in my head of John then turning to say much the same thing to, well, no one, then following us all back up the stairs while calling out to Phorn.

It all seemed so absurd that we started laughing again, and the higher we climbed, heading in the wrong direction, the more we laughed. It was as if we all now had a death wish. I could hear the theme to *Towering Inferno* playing over and over in my head, 'We May Never Love Like This Again'. Suddenly I found myself singing it out loud. How did I even know this song? It was crazy, I'd never been a fan of Maureen McGovern.

'Stop singing that please, Jimmy,' Jane shot back at me. She had a stern Shelley Winters look on her face. Weirdly, Shelley wasn't even in *Towering Inferno*, but I always think of her when there's a major disaster.

FOR WHOM THE BELL TOLLS

We made it back to the twenty-sixth floor and into the apartment, and found Jane's mum sitting on a chair holding another, bulkier bag. It seemed that this was where she kept her jewellery.

John came into the room puffing and panting, looked around and was about to grab Phorn by the arm when the alarm stopped.

Suddenly you could have heard a pin drop. John tilted his head towards the speaker in the roof. Would it start up again? Not a sound.

'I told you there was no fire, John,' Phorn said as she picked up her magazine and calmly resumed reading from where she'd left off.

I had a similar experience one time we were on tour in Scotland in the late 1990s, when, in the middle of the night, fire alarms started ringing out through the hotel we were staying at in Glasgow. It was part of the Malmaison chain co-founded by Mick Hucknall, the frontman of the band Simply Red. To me, Simply Red owning hotels seemed like a great idea, because I fell asleep every time I listened to them.

On this particular night, it was cold and rainy, and it felt like it was on the verge of snowing as I walked back into the hotel. Yes, it was a summer night in Scotland.

Funnily enough, Jane's mum was on tour with us at the time. We said goodnight in the foyer and headed to our respective rooms. One hour later, when I was in the middle of a deep, deep sleep, Jane shook me awake.

'The alarm is going off, Jimmy. We'd better get out of the room and see what's happening.'

I realised that meant I'd better get up and see what was happening while she stayed warm in bed. So that's what I did. In the hallway I met up with one of the staff, who was shouting, 'Everybody out of the hotel as fast as possible, please.'

'Hold on, just hold on a minute,' I joked, 'it's not that bad. I've stayed in much worse hotels than this. Anyway, if you felt like that, you should have told us when we checked in.'

He didn't smile at all. Clearly, he had no time for a show-off idiot like me making inappropriate jokes at such a serious time. Which was odd considering who owned the hotel. I thought he would have had a sense of humour. But no, it seemed that this was a real emergency.

I ran back to the room to find Jane and her mum ready by the door. The hotel was a rabbit warren of small corridors divided by fire doors, and no one wanted to be trapped in there if there really was a fire. We made our way in an orderly fashion to the front door and out onto the street. By this point it felt like the rain really had turned to sleet, and I was standing outside in my shorts – it was summer after all – looking up at the sky, holding back the tears, and telling whoever was listening up there that if this was a false alarm I would need all my strength to stop me burning down the hotel myself.

After about half an hour of waiting and shivering, we were told to go back to our rooms. It seemed that someone had ordered room service and the smoke was the result of them asking for burnt toast and not simply bread.

Okay, I made that last bit up.

# The Little Brick House

In my mind, there are places that never let me go. They always rise out of the past and pull me back – in waking thoughts, dreams and even nightmares.

Try as I might to expunge these memories, they are always there. And I know they always will be. Of all the places that do this to me, none is more powerful and persistent than that modest brick home on Heytesbury Road, Elizabeth West, that my family moved into in 1963, a couple of years after our arrival in Adelaide as immigrants from Scotland. Seemingly innocuous sights, smells and sounds can conjure up that home in seconds, bringing with it an overwhelming tide of emotion.

Why does the little brick house have such a hold on me? I guess it's because, for me and my family, at the start it was a place that had so much potential, somewhere that filled us with so much hope. When we got there, happiness seemed to be within reach. And then, somehow, it slipped away, to be replaced by crushing despair.

I hate remembering that pain, reliving that disappointment and heartbreak over and over again, but nothing I do seems to eradicate it. The simple sight of a waterlogged road or field might immediately transport me back to the day we arrived in Heytesbury Road during a torrential downpour. As I've recounted elsewhere, the house was part of a new city being built from the ground up for immigrants, the city of Elizabeth. A city of dreams – our dreams. The muddy roads around the freshly constructed houses were mere bush tracks and looked like they had been recently bombed. There were troughs so

246

The front porch of the little brick house, where life took so many twists and turns. That's me and Alan with Mum, and some neighbours at left.

deep – gouged into the dark red earth by builders' trucks – that you might have disappeared in them. And after all the rain, they were full of water and mud, making it almost impossible for my dad to drive the car up that road without getting bogged.

But as we approached our new neighbourhood, peering through the raindrops relentlessly battering the windscreen, we were nevertheless full of hope. The dreams that had taken us halfway around the world seemed to be coming true. This was where the old life ended and a new life would begin. That's what Mum and Dad had promised us the whole time our boat had struggled to make its way through the relentless storms we'd met head-on as we crossed the Indian Ocean, and through those two years we'd spent living in crummy, claustrophobic hostels. The house in Heytesbury Road would be our house, and nothing, not even a canyon full of sludge, would stop us from reaching it. And now we were almost there.

Sometimes I see vivid images of us arriving at the house, stepping over puddles, walking through the door, then running around the rooms, whooping with delight. Yet my mum always told me I fell asleep in the car just before we got there, and that she carried me inside and put me to bed. Strange the tricks memory can play.

But I'll never forget the excitement I experienced on waking the next day. The rain had cleared and the sun shone. The little brick building immediately felt like a proper home, something we'd never had before. The smell of freshly painted walls will always be the scent of that fresh start for me. Though the muddy yard was scattered with wooden offcuts and mounds of gravel left by the builders, and empty paint cans were stacked against the recently built walls, the outside of the building was trim and clean, the bricks new and pristine, not covered in soot like our Glasgow tenement.

A few days later, when the rain returned, I noticed for the first time a noise like a thousand military drums playing at once. As the raindrops pelted down onto the silver corrugated-iron roof, I thought to myself that nothing had ever sounded this good. I marched through the house in time to the beat. Even to this day, I still love that sound.

The old houses we'd lived in before this had seemed to soak up every sound that was made. The silence was deafening at times. I don't remember ever previously hearing the rain on a roof or the birds in the trees. No noise came in and no noise went out. No one ever heard my mum's screams as she fought with my father, and no one ever heard the sound of us children crying ourselves to sleep each night. Those houses were like tombs, whereas this one was new and alive and waiting for us, and our voices bounced off the walls as we ran joyfully from room to room.

There in that little brick house with its roof made of tin, we all settled down and hoped for a life that was normal. We didn't want any more dramas. Any more fights. Any more tears. And for a while it seemed that might even happen.

Dad and Mum even promised us that we would have a garden and grow our own vegetables. At the start they kept these promises, and they both worked hard to make things right for us. They fed the soil and watered the plants, and new shoots began to push their way through the dirt. But a garden needs constant care and endless nurturing. It needs love and attention. Just like a family.

Before too long, Mum and Dad forgot about the garden. The fresh shoots that had started to grow soon withered and died. Trouble came knocking at our door again. It was like an old friend, and Mum and Dad just opened the door and let it in. They began drinking too much, and they found friends just like the ones they'd had back in Scotland, the ones who scared us kids, and the same old fights started happening again. It appeared our parents' lives were not complete without trouble.

The walls were no longer pristine and white, but full of holes from punches thrown in fits of rage and smeared with dirt and blood. The little brick house wasn't a safe place to be anymore. I took to sitting in the paddock across the road and staring at the house, asking myself what had gone wrong.

Soon our parents couldn't wait to escape too and were constantly looking for reasons to walk out the door. We'd hear it slam, and huddle in a corner, wondering if they'd ever come back. Eventually we were taken away from our little brick house once and for all, and for years were passed from place to place. We never again found the home that had been promised to us.

As an adult with a family, I was determined that none of my children would experience such insecurity and disappointment. With Jane, I'm happy to say that I managed to create a home just like the one I'd prayed for as a child. It has always been warm and safe, and my children have never had to worry about where their next meal is coming from. I can go home and put my feet up, and sit and contemplate how far I have come and, more importantly, how far I still have to go, knowing that my children will never have to feel the way I did. They will always have a good home to come back to, where they are loved, and Jane and I will always be there for them.

Perhaps in response to my parents' failure to tend their garden, we have cultivated a love of nature, plants and growing our own food. I am still not really a gardener, but between Jane and me we keep a good eye on what we are growing. The garden is not a burden to us; it is a gift. All through the year, we are lucky enough to bring fresh organic vegetables into the kitchen to cook for the family. With a little love and attention, my roses bloom every year – I think it's because I walk around talking and singing to them, but that's only my theory. Our house is often filled with the smell of freshly cooked food and the scents from the garden. Each time I walk through the door, I close my eyes and breathe in deeply. I am home: life is good.

And yet. Having attained such comfort and harmony at home, having raised a brood of happy and contented kids, I'm still haunted by what happened at Heytesbury Road. I would love to break its spell and escape those painful recollections. I hoped writing about it in previous books might set me free, and it did to some extent. And I know from the many messages I've received from readers that those stories resonated and even helped others come to terms with their pasts. But the memories, and the nightmares, still return.

I thought perhaps it might help to see the house again and, as I've recounted, a few times when I have been passing through the area I have sat in the car across the street – where the paddock once met the road and where I would hide as a young man and try to make sense of my life – and quietly observed our old home. The little brick house seems quiet and nice these days. I don't know for sure, but it looks like a good family have shared a decent life there as they've grown up. The people, the place, the times have moved on. But in my mind those days still linger, and in moments of anger I sometimes imagine one day buying the little brick house and tearing it down, so that it no longer exists and I never have to see it again.

Recently, I tried to exorcise these ghosts by writing a song, which I'm sure will turn up on an album soon. It's a simple song that starts:

> A small brick house in a sea of mud,
> The rain fell so hard, it surely would flood.
> This was the home that we never had,
> Full of hope and changes, good and bad.

Perhaps being able to express these emotions in song – scream them out as forcefully as possible or turn them into a lament for those lost dreams – might expel them forever. Only time will tell, but at least the house that haunted me all my life is inspiring me to make music, and I think the little brick house would be happy with that.

# The Future Calling

There was not one cloud in the sky that morning as I walked across the field at the end of our road. Our street looked like every other street in the town.

Neat white fences separated each well-kept garden and perfectly proportioned red-brick house from the next. Each yard had the same neatly manicured lawn and the same concrete driveway that led from the mailbox at the front gate to the carport. Everyone knew everyone. When I walked the streets, neighbours would call out, 'Hey, Tommy, how are your mum and dad?' I'd smile, mutter, 'Fine,' and walk on.

My parents had been brought up to believe they were no better than anyone else, but secretly they were terrified of being just like their neighbours. Dad had never seen himself living in suburbia, but here he was, and Mum, she'd always had delusions of grandeur. She wanted to live in the best house in the best street, and she didn't just want to keep up with the neighbours, she wanted to leave them all behind. She wanted her life to be special.

But all the dreams she and Dad had started out with had long since gone by the wayside. Dad had ended up working as a house painter. Every day, he was up with the sun and out of the house before Mum and I even woke up, and he wouldn't get back until at least dinner time. By then he was too tired to even talk to us. He spent his life perfecting other people's houses, helping build *their* dreams, not his – and certainly not Mum's. She just stayed home all day and tried not to think about all the things they'd never do.

To compensate, Mum channelled her energy into keeping the house spotlessly clean. Every day when Dad was out, she wiped, washed or vacuumed every surface, working her way from one end of the house to the other. Then she'd look around and catch sight of something out of place and head back in the opposite direction, wiping, washing and vacuuming again until everything was immaculate. Even then she'd stare back across the room with that look she always seemed to have in those days. Disappointment.

And then Dad would come home from work, tired and hungry, kick off his muddy shoes at the door and walk across her freshly vacuumed floor, leaving large, Yeti-like footprints on her impeccably hoovered carpet. Next, he'd slump down in his filthy work clothes on her newly Scotchgarded couch and put his sweaty feet up on her perfectly polished coffee table. I'm sure he didn't do it to annoy her, he was just worn out, but Mum would yell and scream at him anyway, and then Dad would slowly get up and tidy his mess. Every day, exactly the same thing. It drove Dad crazy, and he even asked her to see a doctor about it, but she just went quiet and started looking for something else to wipe.

I didn't pay much attention to all of this, until the school holidays started and I was at home alone with her. Then it became exhausting.

'Don't put that cup there, Tommy. I just wiped that table.'

'It's a table, Mum. That's what it's for.'

Ignoring me, she'd search obsessively for blemishes on the surface, which was so shiny you could see your face in it. 'Look, there, you've left a mark on it. Let me get my cloth before it stains the wood.'

She was relentless, and I was soon spending all my time trying not to upset her flawless, polished world. That's why I'd started getting up early each morning and walking for an hour or two on my own before I had to face her.

On this particular day, I'd left as the sun rose, before anyone else in the house, even Dad, had stirred. I just threw on some clothes, grabbed my phone and tip-toed out of the house.

In the field at the end of the street, the sea of long, wild grasses swished hypnotically around my legs. Magpies warbled, greeting the day, and one swooped past my head to remind me I was getting too close to its nest. A cockatoo squawked and drifted across the sun, throwing a shadow onto the dry, cracked ground beyond the field. I looked up, squinting while trying to focus my eyes on the beautiful crested bird as it soared on the wind, high above my head. I followed it across the sky until it was nothing but a small white speck that then disappeared into the distance.

I walked along a corrugated-iron fence that led me to another road and the endless rows of houses of the next suburb. And that was when I first heard it: music, floating in the air, soft and low. Different from the music my mum played at home, her slow, monotonous old music that put me to sleep. And not like any of the loud, scabrous music Dad played in the car, songs he'd sing along with after he'd drunk too much beer. No, this music was melodic, intricate and full of life, and it floated around me like smoke from a fire.

I walked slowly down the street in search of the source of these harmonious sounds. As I reached a corner, I saw a man watering his garden. Though he was frail-looking, he seemed to move elegantly in time with the music, not dancing to it, but swaying as if it was a part of him. He was wearing a broad-brimmed hat that shielded his face from the burning sun, and below its brim I could see a man who was too old to be working in the garden in this heat. He was wrinkled and worn and could have been a hundred, though something about his movements and gestures made him seem younger. Plus he was dressed like someone half his age, in shorts and a black T-shirt printed with what looked like a poster from a rock concert. I could only make out the word *Montreux* in bold print.

As I neared him, I tried my best not to stare, but I was still being drawn to the mysterious melodies, which seemed to be coming from the open window of his house. Captivated by the soft, soaring guitar sounds that were now dancing all around me, I stopped briefly.

'Can I help you?' he asked.

I turned and found him standing close to me and looking at me intently. His eyes were bright and warm.

'Can I help you?' he repeated. 'You look a little lost.'

I wasn't expecting to have a conversation with anyone that morning. And here I was standing in front of a man who looked like he had taken all that the world could throw at him yet was still upright and ready for more. I didn't know what to say.

'You like that?'

I wasn't sure what he meant. 'I'm sorry?' I replied.

'The song.' He turned and looked towards the window. 'Do you like that music?'

'Er, y-y-yes, I do.'

'That's "Days of Wine and Roses" by Wes Montgomery.'

'It's beautiful. I've never heard anything like it before.'

'Well, I'm not surprised. It's from before your time. Johnny Mercer and Henry Mancini wrote that tune back in 1962. That's when they used to write real songs. Not cussing and swearing every second word like they do now. Just sweet melodies that make you think about the world being a better place than it really is. But, hey, I'm getting ahead of myself now. My name's George. What's yours, son?'

'My name is Tommy. Tommy Valentine.'

'I used to know a guitar player in the fifties with a name like that. You ever played a guitar?'

'No, sir. My mum says she wants me to play the recorder and Dad wants me to play rugby, but no guitar.'

'Hold on right there a minute. Don't do it. I mean, I'm sure your mum means well, but no one really wants to play the recorder, do they? That's something that's just not right. Music is supposed to feed your soul. Playing the recorder is like being starved. It's just not good for you. And don't get me started on rugby. One wrong tackle and you might never dance again. Imagine that.'

'I guess so. I never thought about it like that.'

'That's the point: you've got to think about the music you listen to and the things you want to do in this life. And you've got to do even more thinking before you decide what instrument you're going to play. That's a life-changing choice right there. Music can make the sun shine on a rainy day, or it can bring you down faster than an elevator.'

'I guess if it was up to me I'd play the guitar, I think. But my parents won't let me.'

I could hear a strange scraping sound, repeating over and over. I glanced towards the window.

'You want to hear more? I can play something else for you.'

'Yeah, sure, if you've got time. Er, what is that noise?'

'That, dear boy, is the sound of a vinyl record reaching the end of side one. You know what vinyl is? Probably not. You guys have MP3s or streaming or something like that. Vinyl is the way that you're supposed to hear music. If God wanted you to stream, he wouldn't have given us record players. A stream is something you lie next to with your girl on a summer's day. I tell you what, just sit yourself down on the step here and I'll play you some sounds that will blow your mind. You ever heard of Jim Hall or Django Reinhardt?'

'No, sir, I haven't.'

'Okay, let's get one thing straight, Tommy. You can lose the "sir". My name's George. My friends used to call me Guitar George.'

He muttered something about 'back in the day' under his breath as he went into the house. I heard a boom and a loud crackling noise, then music filled the air again. George walked back through the doorway, smiling, and sat down next to me on the front porch. The warm morning sun shone on us as we listened to the music. He swayed and tapped his foot in time to each song and told me stories about leaving home and travelling the country, playing guitar in a jazz band. It was funny, but he looked younger now he was talking about music. Much younger than he'd seemed when I first saw him alone in the garden.

'Do they still call you Guitar George?'

'No, son. Not anymore. All my friends are gone. Me and my band played our last set quite a few years ago. Probably before you were born. No, it's just me left now. Eddie Eighty-Eight played the piano in the band – you know there are eighty-eight keys on a piano, dontcha?'

I nodded, even though I hadn't known that.

'He was as good as anyone I ever met. Never seen anybody better since either, now that I think of it. He died in a car crash in the winter of seventy-seven. He was heading to a gig somewhere up the North Coast and he fell asleep at the wheel. The car was written off, but they told me music was still blasting from the car's cassette deck when they found him wrapped around that tree. It was Bill Evans, I believe. That was the way he would have wanted to go. On the road, doing shows.'

He paused, seemingly lost in thought. I stared at my trainers and waited for him to continue.

'Then there was Big Joe Murray, one of the greatest trumpet players of all time, in my opinion. Man, he could blow up a storm on that horn, but he doesn't even remember my name now. He's still alive, but he ain't living, if you know what I mean. These days he's in an old folks' home, wearing nappies, not knowing what's going on, and someone has to spoon-feed him mashed food to keep him alive. I took his horn in to him a while back, but he didn't know one end from the other. It broke my heart. They should just let him go peacefully.'

I thought I saw a tear in the corner of his eye. But then he seemed to brighten again.

'Slapping Jack Malone played the bass. Every single night he would make his double bass sound like a freight train rolling down the track. That is until the night he went missing. We were on tour in the Western Australian goldfields, playing jazz for the miners. I remember it well. We played a bunch of great shows out in the red dust there. The crowds went crazy. Those miners loved us. Every night after we finished we went back to our hotel to sleep it off. Jack and me, we shared a room. On the third day I woke up and he was gone. I thought he'd taken a walk or something. His bass was sitting in the corner of the room where he'd left it and his bag was next to his bed. He didn't come back and I never heard from him again. I tried to hunt him down around the traps, but he'd just disappeared off the face of the planet. I miss old Jack.'

He smiled as if remembering a joke they'd once shared.

'Two-Ton Tony Tamahi was on the skins – that's what we called the drums. He moved here from New Zealand to make a living playing drums in the early sixties, but no one really made a living playing music, they just did it because they loved it. Tony could swing like a rusty old gate in the wind, but then one day he dropped dead from a heart attack. The doctors had told him he had to lose weight and stop drinking, but Tony liked the good life. Too much beer and too much fried chicken. And he wasn't giving up either for no doctor. No son, now they're all gone but me.'

George's eyes glazed over as he thought of them. Then he said, 'Let me play you something else. You ever listen to Miles Davis.'

'Not that I know of.'

'Well, you haven't lived. You've got to hear him. Sit back and take a load off your feet, and let me take you on a cool jazz trip.'

I sat on the front porch of Guitar George's house for hours and listened to song after song. With every tune I got another story. Stories about the road, the music, the highway wide open in front of you, and never looking in the rearview mirror.

'You've got to keep moving forward in this life, Tommy. No regrets. Leave it all on the road.'

Before I knew it, the morning had drifted by and my stomach was rumbling like one of Two-Ton Tony's tom-toms. I suddenly remembered Mum would expect me to be home in time to do my chores, so I stood up. 'I have to go, but I'd love to come by again tomorrow and hear some more music if you're not too busy.'

'Busy. Ha! No, I'm not busy. Not anymore. Anytime you like, boy. I've still got a little time left in this world and I can't think of anything I'd rather do with it than play music to a young fella like you. Maybe I can show you my guitar, Jezebel. That's her name. Best guitar I ever had. I could make that old girl sing like an angel.'

'Yes, that'd be great. I think I really want to be a guitar player now.'

'Okay then, son, see you same time tomorrow.'

I went back every day for a week. And every day Guitar George told me more stories about touring and travelling. About music and how it can save your soul. And he kept promising to introduce me to Jezebel, but then would forget.

Still, each morning after seeing George, I woke up feeling completely rested. I'd forgotten about all the problems I had at home; in fact, I hadn't slept so well in years. Every night I dreamed about guitars playing soft, low, crisp chords, and what I'd learned were called arpeggios, played by nimble fingers that rhythmically danced along smoke-stained fretboards.

Then one morning I woke up and walked into the kitchen. Mum was clearing the breakfast dishes from the table.

'You slept in late, son. Must have been tired out after all your walking. Dad's gone to the garage to fill up the car. He thinks we should go away for a few days to the sea. It'll do us all good.'

I liked the idea of a family holiday, but in my heart I wanted to stay home, as I'd made plans to meet George again. But I had little say in the matter.

Three days later, we pulled back into the driveway of our house, refreshed and smiling. The break did seem to have been good for Mum and Dad. The sea air had lifted Mum's spirits, she was laughing like a young girl, and she looked beautiful. But I had a feeling that might not last long.

Next morning I woke up early and ran out of the house. I wanted to hear more of George's music and his stories, and finally meet Jezebel. As I turned the corner to his house, I was shocked to see an ambulance pulling into the driveway. I ran to the front door but was stopped by a man coming from inside.

'Has something happened to George? What's wrong?' I asked.

The man looked at me. His eyes were red and bloodshot. He'd been crying, I could tell.

'Who are you, son?'

'My name's Tommy.'

'Oh, so you're Tommy Valentine. I've heard a lot about you from George. You made quite an impression on him. He said you reminded him of his young self. I'm George Junior. Guitar George was my daddy, Tommy.'

'What do you mean "was"? Is everything all right?'

'Yes, Tommy, everything is cool. Guitar George has left the building.'

'What do you mean?'

'George died last night, in his sleep.'

This was too much. I began to cry too.

'Hey, no need for tears. He was ready to go. He told me before he went to bed last night that it was time to move on to his next gig. He's somewhere else playing music now, Tommy. If you give me your folks' phone number, I'll let you know when his funeral will be. He didn't want much, just a few songs before he hits the road.'

I gave him our phone number then turned and started to walk home. I was sad but also had a feeling, deep inside my heart, that George would now be free. Just like when he was on tour.

As I walked away, I heard my name being called. I looked back and saw George Junior running after me. In his hand was a large weather-beaten case. As he neared, I saw it was covered in stickers and when I looked more closely I realised there had to be one from nearly every town in Australia.

'Before George went to sleep last night, he told me to find you and give you this. He said you were going to need it.'

I opened the case. Inside was the most beautiful thing I had ever seen.

'Her name is Jezebel.'

'Wow ... I mean ... I know. I heard a lot about her.'

'Well, she's yours now, Tommy.'

I was astonished. I stared in wonder at this beautiful object, and I swear I saw my future in it.

And so it was. As soon as I was old enough, I left home and joined a band, just like George had done.

I have never looked back.

# Jazz Greats

| | |
|---|---|
| 'Days of Wine and Roses' | WES MONTGOMERY |
| *Kind of Blue* (whole album) | MILES DAVIS |
| 'Take Five' | DAVE BRUBECK QUARTET |
| 'Skating in Central Park' | BILL EVANS AND JIM HALL |
| 'Django's Tiger' | DJANGO REINHARDT |
| 'Blue in Green' | BILL EVANS |
| 'Lullaby of Birdland' | ELLA FITZGERALD |
| 'Autumn Leaves' | JOE PASS |
| 'Bright Size Life' | PAT METHENY |
| 'But Beautiful' | STAN GETZ AND BILL EVANS |
| 'Midnight Blue' | KENNY BURRELL |
| 'I Put a Spell on You' | NINA SIMONE |
| 'Strange Fruit' | BILLIE HOLIDAY |
| 'The Girl from Ipanema' | ASTRUD GILBERTO |

# Old Haunts

When outsiders visit Scotland, spending a night in a castle is often at the top of their wish list, and there are certainly plenty of places on offer.

If you get it right it can be a wonderful, romantic and thrilling experience. There's really nothing better than sinking into a bed covered with a doona that is so stuffed with goose feathers that it looks about three feet thick, or sitting in a plush velvet armchair, surrounded by antiques, sipping piping-hot hot chocolate, while you settle into a good book and the rain whips sideways past small, cross-shaped windows designed to keep arrows out. And I love that sense of travelling back in time to another period of history. But get it wrong and it might just be cold and chilling, and it could even leave you looking for a way out, in the depths of a dark, dark night.

I booked a castle once, sight unseen, for Jane and me on one of our many trips back to my old homeland. We wanted to share the Scottish experience with her dear mum and dad, Phorn and John, who were travelling with us at the time. Jane's parents were seasoned travellers and were ready for any adventure. The castle offered long walks in the garden, which I knew they would love. Lessons in hunting with a bow and arrow were available too. You never know when such skills might come in handy, but I wasn't keen on giving Phorn and John medieval weapons in case they weren't happy with my booking. Fortunately, they weren't interested in that activity, or the castle's main attraction, a falconry course. This involves teaching guests how to catch food using a vicious-looking bird of prey that has to have its eyes covered most of the time so it doesn't turn on you. Now I'm all for catching my own food, but I don't want any mangy old peregrine way past its prime sticking its beak into my dinner before I sink my teeth into it, so I vetoed that idea well before we got there.

When we arrived at the castle, which was basically a round fort attached to a new awning where they had built some function rooms for conventions, my first thoughts were: 'Oh, it's a lot smaller than I expected. I hope they have large rooms.' But at least the original building seemed authentic – it even had a drawbridge, though it looked a bit decrepit.

As we walked in, though, I was suddenly overcome with a deep sense of fear. I noticed the walls were hung with a range of medieval torture devices. Or were they marital aids from the Middle Ages? I wasn't sure, and I wasn't keen to find out.

While we checked in, an old man wearing a kilt lurked in the shadows of the entrance hall, yabbering away to no one in particular. We were told he'd bring our luggage up in due course, so we headed to our rooms. The walls were cold and all the stairwells seemed to lead to darkness. Some had signs for dining rooms and other facilities, but I was convinced they all led to dungeons. I'm not great with scary places – most of my life I have been scared for one reason or another, so it's the last thing I need to feel on a holiday. I wanted to turn around and get far away from the place as soon as possible, but Jane calmly said, 'Just wait a minute. It might be better once we're in the room.'

We found our door, unlocked it and peered in. Shadows danced across the dimly lit walls, immediately playing tricks with my overly active imagination. I got the feeling that the rooms were themed, and I was fairly sure ours was Ye Old Drawn and Quartered Suite. I turned on every lamp in the place, but there still wasn't enough light to even read the fire-escape plans that showed the way to the nearest exits. We really were back in the Dark Ages.

A huge four-poster bed, covered in red velvet to hide the bloodstains, I figured, filled most of the room, and the walls were decorated with tapestries depicting battles fought in close proximity to the very building we were staying in.

Jane and her parents were reluctant to leave. They seemed quite happy to spend the night in this haunted place and get to know the ghosts that roamed the corridors. But not me. I sat at the desk by the window for a moment, considered our options, then quickly turned around and walked back down to the entrance hall, past the loquacious lord in the kilt, through the very heavy and extremely creaky front door, across the dodgy drawbridge and into the car. I was gone before anyone could ask, 'Excuse me,

When you find the right castle, it's magical. Me and my girl, dressed for dinner at Skibo Castle, near Dornoch, in the north of Scotland.

is my head missing?' And soon the others, much more slowly, followed.

They say a man's home is his castle, but this one was definitely not my castle or my home, so off we went in search of new, ghost-free accommodation. I was looking for a more modern castle, maybe even a stately home. I didn't want much, just the kind of place where opinionated world leaders relax and drink lashings of fifty-year-old single-malt whisky in front of roaring log fires in huge drawing rooms adorned with portraits of stern-faced old men just like them, while discussing global problems and how to ignore them.

Fortunately, I knew of such a place and it wasn't far away. Well, nothing's far away in Scotland, especially compared to Australia, where you can drive for five hours and still be on the same property. Within an hour, we pulled into beautiful Gleneagles, a grand and historic hotel set on a sprawling country estate, surrounded by perfectly manicured golf courses, in the hills of Perthshire. It still gives you that feeling of being in a castle, without the remnants of misery and suffering clinging to almost every wall left behind from the Middle Ages, or the last owners. We've visited many times, and I've always felt right at home there.

All that said, the golf courses are as brutal and torturous as anything the Middle Ages could offer up – I've played there often enough to know I need to carry a calculator to add up my score. But there would be no golf on this trip; the Scottish summer had made sure of that. Following days of torrential rain, the fairways were knee-deep in water. So we'd just have to make do with relaxing, eating good food and being pampered.

Opening my eyes at dawn next morning to the sound of bagpipes being played beside the loch that now covered the lawn below my window was a highlight for me. I sprang out of bed and readied myself for a full Scottish breakfast. I thought seriously of doing a good work-out so I could eat more, but decided to just enjoy the breakfast then hop back into bed and read the newspaper. As I entered the dining room, I could tell from across the room that not all of our party had appreciated the bagpipes as much as I had. Apparently, when he heard them, Jane's father, John, had leaped from the bed screaming.

He was still not happy. 'Did you hear that noise this morning? What a racket. It sounded like there was a cat being murdered below my window. Bloody bagpipes, they should only be played once a year, at the Edinburgh Tattoo.'

I got the impression he would have been more content to share the sunrise with the ghosts and ghouls that clearly ran around our previous choice of accommodation than with the Highland piper on the lawn that morning.

I, on the other hand, was full of beans – or at least would be soon. I started my big breakfast with porridge served with cream and brown sugar. It was delicious and more than enough for a normal human. But the waiter assured me in his thick Scottish brogue that I needed more than that to face the typical summer weather that was waiting for us outside. I wasn't going to have my manhood challenged by a waiter or a hotel breakfast, so I went the whole hog.

What followed can only be described as crazy. Black pudding (beef or pork blood mixed with suet and oats), white pudding (pork with suet and oats), square sausage, bacon, fried eggs, fried tomatoes and baked beans, topped with 'tattie' scones. Tattie scones are mashed potatoes mixed with flour and butter, then flattened into triangular pancakes and fried in bacon fat and butter. I could feel my arteries blocking up as they placed the monster plateful down on the table. Jane looked at it with disgust.

Thirty minutes, and three cups of tea later, breakfast was finally over. I managed to haul myself up the stairs and roll back to our room, where I fell on the bed and slept for an hour. There would be no exercise for me that morning, unless it involved a stomach pump.

The plan for the day was to drive up into the hills and catch a glimpse of the bonny purple heather we had heard about in so many quaint Scottish folk songs. So, just before midday, we prepared to set off on our adventure.

'I'm sure this weather is going to clear up fer ye. Ye'll have a bonny day, so ye will,' said the concierge with a laugh as we piled into the car, wrapped in tartan blankets. Having loaded a picnic handily supplied by the hotel, we headed along a winding country road that was only just wide enough for one car. I was thinking that if by chance we met someone coming the other way, we'd have to reverse all the way back to the hotel or overpower the occupants of the other car and roll their vehicle into the misty wee glen by the road so we could continue. Luckily there was no one else on the road that day. That might have had something to do with the rain that was coming down in waves so strong that we feared the car would be washed off the road, or the fog that made it so hard to see that we had to drive at five miles an hour, or the cold that cut right through to our bones as soon as we opened the car door.

We drove slowly west until we reached what the map said was the side of Ben Vorlich, a sizable local mountain where the hotel had recommended a picnic spot. But the weather had now got even worse and we couldn't even see the side of the road let alone the top of the mountain. We set up base camp in the car with the engine running, so as not to freeze to death, and, without a word being spoken, we quietly ate our picnic. I got the feeling the hotel had provided it in case we never made it back, and it was meant to keep us alive until the search party found us.

'Hey guys, why don't we go to Italy again,' I said as cheerfully as I could, considering my lips were stuck together and my fingers were falling off due to frostbite. I honestly think that summer trips to Scotland should be accompanied by free one-way tickets to Italy so you can thaw out after your visit.

Next trip, I think I will take Jane and her mum and dad to stay at the Gritti Palace in Venice. At least the water is supposed to be there, and they give you a boat to get around.

# Our Precious Time

We never have enough time. You think you have nothing but time on your side, then it suddenly catches up to you and runs you down.

Time tests us, taunts us, and even tempts us. You think: if I can just move things around, I will have a little more time and then I can catch up and get back on track. But you seldom do. We talk about how precious time is to us, then a moment later we go out and waste so much of that same priceless commodity. It's a sin. Grains of sand that have slipped through the hourglass are gone forever, as if blown away in the wind. In our youth, time stretches out in front of us, endless, then settles into a steady rhythm, tricking us into complacency, leading us to ignore its passing along with the many precious moments, opportunities and friendships that are surely lost and wasted. Before we know it, we're running out of time faster than we're running out of road.

Back in the 1960s, in the bleak industrial towns of northern Britain, poverty and unhealthy living conditions meant that for many people time was short. You hadn't been given a lot of it, so if you had dreams, you had to make the most of your time, and soon. And in those days it seemed that as long as you stayed in Britain, those dreams would never be fulfilled.

So it was for our family, and so it was for the family of Steve Prestwich, who'd been born not so far from my home in Glasgow, in the similarly tough, industrial city of Liverpool. These were manufacturing and shipbuilding towns whose industries had declined rapidly in the postwar era. At almost the same time, our families realised that their clocks were ticking and decided to emigrate to Australia to give their children the best chance of making the most of their lives. Without ever meeting, both families travelled over twelve thousand miles across the sea, far from our homes, and as fate would have it, ended up living in the same town, Elizabeth in South Australia. Steve's family settled in Elizabeth East, while we lived in Elizabeth West, no more than five miles away. Steve and I still wouldn't meet for a few years, though our paths probably crossed often on those streets.

I got a little closer to Steve through his young brother, Laurie, a disillusioned young thug like me who hung around with the same gang as I did. We were wild boys who spent a lot of our precious hours drinking, playing pool and fighting. Steve didn't really share those interests – he was a pacifist who had no interest in fighting on the streets – and he made better use of his time, by perfecting his drumming, the one thing he felt would change his life for the better.

Steve came from a musical family. His father had played drums in bands back home in Liverpool and had even played shows in the legendary Cavern Club, the home of The Beatles. So music was in Steve's DNA, and he was always going to play the drums. He had joined bands before he'd left Liverpool, and he soon found his way into the music scene in Elizabeth. He and his band, Ice, were accomplished musicians and they played progressive rock, inspired by that ever-evolving musical style that flourished in the UK in the early seventies. Songs by the likes of Yes and Genesis filled Ice's repertoire, so it's fair to say that their audiences never danced: the complicated rhythms that bubbled below the surface of the songs were too tortuous and difficult to dance to, not without looking like you were having an epileptic fit. Ice were certainly far too progressive for me and my friends, who had mostly been born with two left feet and not much interest in anything progressive, but that didn't mean we didn't appreciate their talent. And we could see that Steve was a born time-keeper.

I wanted to be in bands too, but had no idea how to go about it. I came from a family who liked to sing when they'd had a few drinks, and that's how I started performing. I half-heartedly got involved with bands at school, but never really dreamed I would end up on stage. Then one night after drinking way too much, I found myself getting up and singing with a local band in the Elizabeth community centre.

Steve and I still hadn't properly met at this point, but fate, and time, had plans for us. One day while I was hanging out at the shops, looking for trouble, a young red-headed hippy called Michael, who I'd seen around town, handed me a message asking me if I was interested in trying out for a new band that was looking for a singer. I was tempted, but also afraid of stepping out of my comfort zone, where I was a bigshot among a bunch of dropkicks. 'What if this new band don't like me?' I asked myself.

I decided that if I did go, I wouldn't tell my friends. That way they'd never know if I missed out – I could never have lived down a failure like that. Anyway, it was my own precious time and if I wanted to waste it, so what? Time was something that had been on my mind of late: increasingly, I was aware of my youth passing. The clock was ticking and I had to seize the moment.

I took the train into the city and sheepishly walked to the address I'd been given. The audition would be held at two o'clock in the Women's Liberation Centre, which seemed a funny place to try out for a rock 'n' roll band. I was sure that choice of venue was supposed to send a message to me, but whatever it was flew straight over my head, so I simply put on my leather jacket, puffed out my chest and walked in, on time. I was expecting the worst.

The band were great, although the drummer was a weak point. He had no real sense of rhythm or timing – well, not enough to drive a band. I sang a few songs and then waited for an answer. Did they like me or would I have to crawl back to Elizabeth with my heart filled with shame?

The band were waiting for their moment to shine, and it turned out, much to my surprise, that they wanted me to be a part of that moment. But they'd decided the drummer would have to go. We all started looking around for a replacement. When I quizzed my big brother, John, he suggested that we try a drummer he had seen playing around Elizabeth. 'You'll love this guy, Jim. He swings, he's really good. But I'm not sure what he's up to. His name is Steve Prestwich.'

Our time had come. In October 1973, Steve walked into that Women's Liberation Hall and sat down at his drum kit. As he counted in the first song, something inside me told me this was it, this was the moment. Sure enough, Steve became our drummer, and that vital cog in a band, the time-keeper. A rock 'n' roll band are only as good as their drummer, and Steve was perfect. We had chosen Steve to keep our precious time.

Soon we changed our name from Orange, a terrible name we used to perform our first show, to Cold Chisel, an equally terrible name we would end up stuck with. Within a year Phil Small would join the band, completing the rhythm section, and we were ready to take on the world. Steve and Phil became the linchpin of the band, its beating heart, working hard to keep us on track, though there were times when the momentum of the shows made it difficult even for them to maintain order. Their intricate rhythms, which swirled beneath the surface of the songs, not only drove us along but also made us much more interesting than most other bands in the country.

After that first decade of touring took its toll, the members of Cold Chisel drifted apart. Lost and alone, I fumbled my way through the quagmire that is the music business. I had a lot of success, but I knew something was missing. Then in 1997 Cold Chisel put the years of pain and struggle behind us and decided we had unfinished business. The band re-formed and I felt whole again. Every night as I sang, I could feel that driving force that was my friend Steve, holding the band together. No matter how much I pushed it forward or pulled it back, he fought me and kept the rhythm constant. He was the metronome, constantly ticking in the background, holding time on a tight leash.

Things seemed to be looking up for us. When we found out that Steve had developed a brain tumour, we were of course shocked, and terrified for him as he undertook his first treatments. But he was stoic and tried to reassure us. When he went in for surgery, he brushed off our concerns, told us he'd be fine, back with us before we knew it, promised to call us when he got out. But he never woke up after the operation.

The five members of that band – Don, Ian, Phil, Steve and myself – were brothers. From that day in 1973 when we'd first met Steve, we had been there for each other through thick and thin. Now, Steve, our precious time-keeper was gone.

My heart was broken, but I learned a lot from that tragedy. And since then the sudden loss of other irreplaceable mates who have long been part of my story has reinforced that lesson. We are not here for long, the clock is ticking, and one day our time will run out. We must do everything we can to hold on to our precious time and not let it slip through our fingers, to love and laugh with the people we hold most dear – before it's all gone.

Every second is priceless. Every moment should be cherished.

# Our Steve's Sounds

| | |
|---:|:---|
| 'Ferry Cross the Mersey' | GERRY AND THE PACEMAKERS |
| *Music of My Mind* (whole album) | STEVIE WONDER |
| 'One Love' | BOB MARLEY |
| 'Water into Wine' | COLD CHISEL |
| 'Stop! In the Name of Love' | THE SUPREMES |
| *Talking Book* (whole album) | STEVIE WONDER |
| 'Papa Was a Rollin' Stone' | THE TEMPTATIONS |
| 'Walk Away Renee' | FOUR TOPS |
| 'When the War is Over' | COLD CHISEL |
| 'Boogie on Reggae Woman' | STEVIE WONDER |
| 'The Harder They Come' | JIMMY CLIFF |
| 'What's Going On' | MARVIN GAYE |
| 'Long Distance Runaround' | YES |
| 'Never Dreamed You'd Leave in Summer' | STEVIE WONDER |
| 'Forever Now' | COLD CHISEL |

# Acknowledgements

Everyone thinks writing a book is a lonely task, driven by the writer's need to get his or her stories out, and in some ways it is, but it goes a lot further than that. In fact, it takes a team of dedicated professionals to deliver a book to you, readers. Can you believe that this is my sixth book with HarperCollins? I love this team.

Helen Littleton, my publisher, thank you for giving me my start in the book writing business. It brings me a lot of joy, and I love your encouragement. I was in daily contact with Scott Forbes, managing editor for HarperCollins Adult Books, frequently asking, 'Does this sound right?' or 'Is this too stupid?' So I would like to thank Scott for his patience and guidance.

While I'm at it, I would like to thank Graeme Jones and Fiona Luke for typesetting and prepress work, Pam Dunne for proofreading, Darren Holt for the fabulous design of the cover and internals, Mark Campbell and Rachel Walker for additional design support, and Janelle Garside for her production work. Big love to Karen-Maree Griffiths, who worked on my first book with me and is now Sales Director of HarperCollins, and is about to sell another one for me with her passionate team.

Thanks, too, to all the team at the HarperCollins warehouse, just down the road from me in Moss Vale –

locals, and 'Highlanders' like me, who pick and pack and send out my books to all the retailers. I also want to thank the bookshops all over Australia for years of support. I love a good book and I've been into so many of your shops over the years I feel like we are all old mates.

A lot of the highways and byways I travelled were with my dear friends in Cold Chisel: Don, Ian, Phil, Steve, Charley. We hit the road fifty years ago, playing any dive or bar that would have us and ended up selling out the biggest venues in Australia. Half a century on, we are still exploring new highways and byways. The road goes on forever.

The beautiful cover photo was taken by Jesse Lizotte, my extremely talented nephew. I'm grateful to my close confidants, John Watson and Rina Ferris, who I call constantly to reassure me I am writing good things.

To my darling daughter Mahalia Barnes, who has taken over the reins of the business and now manages me, I love you.

Now that I have put these stories to rest, Jane and I are working furiously on our new cookbook, which is so exciting. It's going to be great, mainly because I'll get to try all of Jane's wonderful food along the way.

Finally, I want to thank you, dear readers, for all your support. I have many more tales to tell you, so I'd better get back to writing them.

Jimmy

Cold Chisel around 1974, playing one of our earliest gigs at the University of New England in Armidale, NSW, where Don was studying.

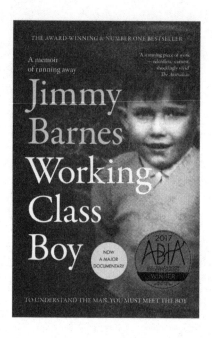

A household name, an Australian rock icon, the elder statesman of Ozrock – there isn't an accolade or cliche that doesn't apply to Jimmy Barnes. But long before Cold Chisel and Barnesy, long before the tall tales of success and excess, there was the true story of James Dixon Swan – a working class boy whose family made the journey from Scotland to Australia in search of a better life.

*Working Class Boy* is a powerful reflection on a traumatic and violent childhood, which fuelled the excess and recklessness that would define, but almost destroy, the rock 'n' roll legend. This is the story of how James Swan became Jimmy Barnes. It is a memoir burning with the frustration and frenetic energy of teenage sex, drugs, violence and ambition for more than what you have.

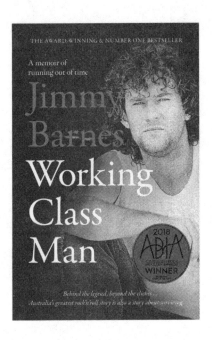

It's a life too big and a story too extraordinary for just one book. Jimmy Barnes has lived many lives – from Glaswegian migrant kid to iconic front man, from solo superstar to proud father of his own musical clan. In this hugely anticipated sequel to his critically acclaimed bestseller, *Working Class Boy*, Jimmy picks up the story of his life as he leaves Adelaide in the back of an old truck with a then unknown band called Cold Chisel.

A spellbinding and searingly honest reflection on success, fame and addiction; this self-penned memoir reveals how Jimmy Barnes used the fuel of childhood trauma to ignite and propel Australia's greatest rock 'n' roll story. But beyond the combustible merry-go-round of fame, drugs and rehab, across the Cold Chisel, solo and soul years – this is a story about how it's never too late to try and put things right.

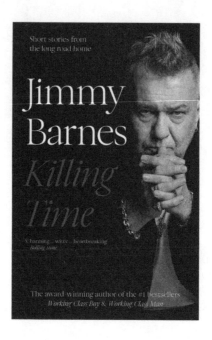

Tales of adventure, misadventure, love and loss – this collection of non-fiction short stories from the Australian rock legend turned writer is vintage Jimmy.

Outrageous, witty, warm and wise, *Killing Time* shares more than forty yarns reflecting an epic life – from an encounter with a soul legend in Memphis, a night in a haunted studio in upstate New York, and a doomed haircut in Thailand to a madcap misunderstanding in a Japanese ski resort, a family feud on a remote coral atoll, and an all-too-revealing appearance for a Sydney charity.

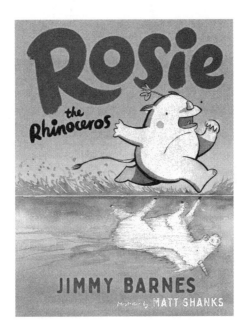

Who is Rosie?

Is she a fun-loving rhinoceros who is always up early and ready to greet the day? Or is she a magical unicorn who skips through the savannah on her dainty hooves?

Either way she's perfect.

From the award-winning author and rock legend Jimmy Barnes and critically acclaimed illustrator Matt Shanks comes a book about the joy of being yourself.

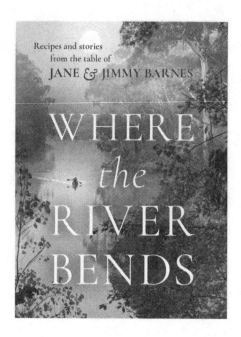

Recipes and stories
from the table of
JANE & JIMMY BARNES

WHERE
the
RIVER
BENDS

Jane and Jimmy Barnes invite you to their kitchen table to share heart-warming stories and favourite dishes ranging from nutritious breakfasts and healthy lunches through classic pastas and Thai curries to Sunday roasts and delectable desserts. Inspired by the food they love and the legendary feasts they host for family and friends, *Where the River Bends* features more than 70 recipes, accompanied by personal recollections and anecdotes and stunning photography.